Slick Lawman

Curly Simpson was after a job but he didn't know just how bad a choice he had made when he signed on at the Pineapple Ranch. He was prepared for a tough outfit and indeed he was mighty handy himself with fist and gun, but this bunch was different. They quickly showed they wouldn't stop at murder if anyone got in their way. Then there was the mystery of why everyone in Ramrod City feared or hated the Pineapple and its ruthless manager Bill Crowe.

Now Curly had to choose his path and wherever he placed his loyalties death would stalk him all the way. He would be without friends both in Ramrod City and at Pineapple Ranch. For all his skills would he be lucky enough to escape branding-iron, bushwhack and bullet?

Slick Lawman

Rick Richards

A Black Horse Western

ROBERT HALE · LONDON

First hardcover edition 2003
Originally published in paperback as
Slick Lawman by V. Joseph Hanson

ISBN 0 7090 7283 X

Robert Hale Limited
Clerkenwell House
Clerkenwell Green
London EC1R 0HT

Typeset by
Derek Doyle & Associates, Liverpool.
Printed and bound in Great Britain by
Antony Rowe Limited, Wiltshire

CHAPTER ONE

The man came down the stairs on his back. Curly Simpson, who was climbing up, turned and made a desperate leap. He hit the bottom a split second ahead of the hurtling body and he back-pedalled. The man squirmed at his feet, tubby, seedy-looking, with rolling eyes.

Curly helped him up. 'No bones broken,' he said.

The man did not say a word but tore himself free and limped rapidly for the door. He reached it, flung it open; it banged behind him.

Curly shrugged and picked up his war-bag. He looked upwards at the big man at the top of the stairs.

'Lookin' f'r somebody?' said the big man in a harsh rumbling voice.

'I was after a room.' Curly walked to the bottom of the stairs and took a few tentative steps upwards.

'Have yuh got the money to pay for it?'

'Wa-al—'

'Whadyuh mean: wa-al? Have yuh or ain't yuh?'

'I ain't – but I could work it off.'

A thumb was jerked: even from where Curly stood it looked big as a baby's hand. 'See that skunk who just left? He couldn't pay f'r his room either.'

'He didn't tell you when he took it?'

'No, he didn't.'

'*I'm* tellin' yuh.'

The big man's round lardy face went a little pink. Curly got ready to duck and run, the body up there looked as big as a bull-buffalo's. Then, surprisingly, a rumble issued from it, blossoming quickly into a full-throated laugh.

'Come on up, pardner.'

Curly advanced tentatively, swinging his war-bag. He was a medium-sized young fellow with homely, cheerfully pugnacious features and a thatch of sandy hair with more kinks in it than a choirboy's.

He looked up at the big man, who seemed to be measuring him, who finally said: 'Could you ride herd on a flock o' dirty dishes?'

He might have said 'or are you too damn' proud' but he didn't, and Curly, who sensed that he was being tested, said: 'I guess so.'

The big man stopped. His eyes, little and black, pouched in lardy fat, glinted with devilment. He was bald, except for a fringe of grey hair, and his smooth pate was as white and greasy as his face. His huge dirty-white apron was in two halves, the waist-string tight and hidden.

'The name's Tiny Waters,' he said. Curly's hand was engulfed in a huge one which felt like a velvet pad, until pressure was exerted, and then the cowboy winced.

Curly did the honours for himself and he learned that Tiny owned the boarding-house and ran the lunch-room in back too.

'How long shall you be wantin' the room for?'

'Until I get a job.'

'Cowhand?'

'Yeh. Shouldn't be hard to get a job around here, uh.'

'It ain't hard,' said Tiny; his deep voice was uncommunicative. He rolled down the passage, with Curly at his heels, and flung open a door at the end.

'This is the only empty room. That skunk I jest threw downstairs bunked here f'r a week. My woman'll clean it. Stash your stuff in a corner for the time bein'.'

'That'll do me fine – thanks. Are you in the habit of throwing folks downstairs?'

'No more'n once a week.'

Curly looked into the smooth round face. There was no humour there but a devil danced in the little black eyes.

'Will you be wantin' chow?'

'Wal yeh. I could do with a filler.'

'It's on now. Through the door back o' the hall … See yuh.' Tiny ambled away.

Curly gave one of his quizzical shrugs and went into the room. He had seen dozens like it. Sagging bed with faded pink counterpane, rickety marble-topped washstand with spotty mirror tacked to the wall above it, basin and pitcher with pink flowers, small chair, bare boards laid with faded mats. Dirty windows, dingy curtains, an atmosphere of fug.

Curly crossed the room. A loose board protested beneath his heavy high-heeled riding boots. He dropped his war-bag into a corner. He opened the window. He crossed to the pitcher and looked into it. It was half-full of greasy-looking water.

He turned at a knock on the door. 'Come in,' he said.

It opened. A grimy old lady in a sack-cloth apron bobbed inside like an inquisitive bird. She carried a mop.

'I've come to do your room, suh,' she said.

'I was gonna wash,' he said, 'but there's no soap and towel.'

'I'll get 'em for yuh, suh,' she said. She left her mop and bobbed out again.

Curly went back to the window and looked out. The day was dull, the sky a leaden blue hanging over the rooftops of the town. Curly looked at the rusty corrugated sheeting side of the place next door, across a narrow alley.

So this was Ramrod City. He felt hemmed in by it. He did not like boarding-house bedrooms, dusty little towns; he much preferred a bed under the stars, the open range or, in his more gregarious moments, a bunkhouse full of snoring men. The country he came through had looked good. Fine beef-growing land, good stuff to work with. He had learned that the biggest ranch, *the* ranch of the territory, was the other side of town. He figured he'd ride out there as soon as possible.

The woman returned with a threadbare towel and a half-cake of yellow soap. Then she left him again and he took off his Stetson, his gun-belt and his kerchief, and had a quick wash.

He left his hat on the bed rail and was going to hang his gunbelt there when he changed his mind. He buckled it around his waist, it had a comforting feel. He knotted his kerchief once more then he crossed to his war-bag, undid the string at the mouth, delved inside and produced a small sack of 'makings'. He dropped this into the top pocket of his leather vest.

Then after a final glance around the room he left it.

As he went along the passage another man came out further down. He was weedy and had brilliant red hair. As he turned Curly saw that he was cross-eyed too. His teeth were gappy and black as he grinned and said: 'Howdy.'

'Howdy,' said Curly.

'You're new here, ain't yuh?'

'Yeh.'

'I'm one o' Tiny's reg'lars. Everybody calls me ''Carrots''— Say, did you see Tiny throw that bum down the stairs?' All this was shot out with the rapidity of a repeater as the two men went down the stairs.

'Yeh, I saw it,' said Curly.

'Tiny's a good-nature gink. He'll give anybody a hand-out if they ask f'r it. But he don't like bein' gyped—'

'Seems like he's purty strict on that point.'

Carrots grinned again. 'You hit it, stranger— Say, you goin' into chow?'

'Yeh.'

'So'm I.'

Carrots led the way across the dingy uncarpeted hall to the door at the back. As he opened it a blast of hot air, heavily laded with the smell of overcooked food, hit them full in their faces.

The lunch-room was long and crammed with tables and benches and humanity. White-aproned waiters dodged around with heavily-laden trays.

Carrots wriggled his lean body into the melee and a rather bewildered Curly followed him as closely as possible . Finally Carrots found them a clear space at the end of a bench.

'We're lucky,' he said. 'Being late an' all. Half the town eats here.'

A waiter came across and Carrots asked him 'what was on'. The man spat out a string of words. Curly did not understand any of them except the last one: the inevitable 'cawfee'.

Carrots made a motion of being sick, so realistically that many of his champing neighbours looked up and glared at him.

'I guess we'd better have that then,' he said.

The waiter looked interrogatively at Curly. Curly shrugged and nodded.

The meal proved to be beef – or maybe it was horseflesh – fried potatoes, and beans – finished off with flapjacks and syrup and thick black sweet coffee which almost made the cowboy's hair straight.

For all that the meal was not unappetising. 'Gosh, who fixes this chow?' said Curly.

'Tiny,' replied Carrots. 'He's the cook, too. Look – there he is.'

The giant was standing in his kitchen doorway surveying the room with his devilish eye. Curly was a little astonished. A man who could run a boarding-house and a cafe, cook for all those people and find time to throw folks downstairs inbetween-whiles was a phenomenon indeed.

'You lookin' for a job, Mister?—' Carrots paused tentatively.

'Call me Curly— Yeh, they tell me there's a big spread hereabouts.'

'The Pineapple.'

'That's it I guess. Kind of a queer name.'

'Tain't as fruity as it sounds.'

Curly looked keenly at his neighbour. Maybe Carrots wasn't really as simple as he seemed to be.

'No? You work for 'em?'

'Not me. Did once. But I ain't the kind to work for the Pineapple. I ain't good enough.'

'How come?'

'It's a little hard to explain to a stranger. You'll find out I guess if yuh aim to go there.' He looked the cowboy up and down but without insolence. 'You'd be good enough for 'em I guess though I'd hafta know you a whole lot better to be sure of that.'

Curly had an idea he did not really mean what he

said. His 'good enough' might mean something entirely different. What kind of men did these Pineapple people want?

'Somep'n queer about those people?'

'Queer? Maybe. All a matter of opinion I guess.' Carrots bent over his plate, finished off his flapjacks. All of a sudden he wasn't so garrulous.

Curly shrugged imperceptibly. He sipped his second cup of scalding coffee, squinting through the steam.

'I work at the livery-stables,' said Carrots suddenly. 'Plenty o' jobs goin' in town. You wouldn't want to take a job in town I guess?'

'Nope. I'm a cowhand.'

'I was a cowhand once,' said Carrots. 'If you want to be a cowhand hereabouts you work for the Pineapple. I don't work for the Pineapple any more so I ain't a cowhand.'

'The Pineapple the only ranch?'

'Yeh, 'cept for one or two homesteaders the other side of town. They're on'y scratchin' – they don't need men. They ain't allowed to have men.'

Curly looked at Carrots. The ugly squint-face was guileless beneath the flaming hair.

'You talk in riddles, friend.'

'Mebbe later on you'll understand me better, Curly.'

The cowboy rose. 'I'll mosey along apiece. See you later.'

Carrots flipped a hand languidly. 'Watch yourself – cowboy.'

Curly shrugged as he crossed the room. Easy come, easy go: he wouldn't worry himself about riddles; a man found the answer to all of 'em sooner or later. He saw Tiny watching him then he passed through the door into the hall.

His room did not look any different to when he left it but the old dame's mop had gone.

Curly clapped his hat on his head and looked out of the window once more. He gave his shrug again, it was a loosening of his whole body: he had no time for melancholy ruminations. He whirled as somebody rapped sharply on the door.

'Come in,' he called.

Tiny came in. Curly figured the big man had moved mighty fast to get up the stairs so soon.

The cowboy grinned: 'Have you come to lead me to that flock o' dishes?' he said.

Tiny did not answer right off. Finally he said: 'I don't push folks like that, pardner. Leastways not if they plain-talk me. You comfortable here?'

'Yes, thanks.'

'Goin' job-huntin'?'

'Yeh.'

'Plenty o' jobs in town.'

Everybody seems mighty keen to get me a job in town, thought Curly. Aloud he said; 'I want a ranch job.'

Tiny said: 'Plenty ranchland here. Takin' yuh war-bag?'

'Nope, I'm leavin' it here till I'm fixed up. Don't worry, I won't gyp yuh.'

13

'I didn't think you would. Just thought I'd ask you.'

Curly wondered why Tiny had not made any mention of the biggest ranch, had not offered to direct him. The big man was turning away, obviously he had finished talking.

'See yuh,' he said, and ambled down the passage. He left the door wide open.

Curly shut it softly behind him. Then he produced the 'makings', sat on the bed, rolled himself a smoke and lit up.

He was still smoking when he went down the stairs and out into the street. The midday break was not yet over. Cayuses dozed at hitching racks, a few people ambled across the dusty street. The air was warm, heavy. Ramrod City, with its false fronts, its clapboard and sheet-iron, looked a sleepy little burg. Prematurely aging, dilapidated, rather sordid – like hundreds of other little towns the length and breadth of the West.

Curly went to the livery-stables and awakened the disgruntled little Mexican. He got his hardworking little paint, forked him and took the trail out of town.

CHAPTER TWO

About a mile out the trail ceased to be a regular lead-on any more. It branched out into a lot of little ribbons, only distinguishable to a plainsman like Curly, and leading off in all directions.

The cowboy realised that the way he came in that morning had been the main trail. Here now was country that had not been broken up by little men, fertile cow country. It delighted his eye and his heart to see it.

He halted his paint. The little beast pranced around a little till he stopped it. Curly studied the ground. He was thinking. He could not grumble about the reception he had received in Ramrod. But nobody had told him anything. The only one who had seemed fair to become communicative had finished up by talking like an Indian medicine man … What now?

He shrugged, turned his horse's head a little. He clucked with his tongue and the little beast moved off once more.

In the distance they espied a small grove of trees and the paint quickened his stride. Curly gave him his head. Hoss-sense, that was the answer, he only wished the little crittur could talk.

About fifteen minutes later they moved through the trees, in a morass of cattle-tracks, and came to the small water-hole.

'All right, dry-belly,' said Curly and dismounted.

The paint stepped daintily through the mud to the edge of the water-hole and drank. He had his fill then looked enquiringly at his master.

'Come on,' said Curly. 'I've got plenty in the canteen.' His lips quirked. 'I'm a real friendly cuss – I even talk to hosses.'

The pony came back to him and he remounted.

'All right, pard,' he said. 'Lead the way.'

The little beast went right on through the trees and, about a mile in front Curly saw the big rocks and just behind them the long squatting row of ranch-buildings – like puppies waiting to pounce.

As he rode nearer his eyes became fixed on a sprawling outcrop of huge rocks. The largest was a tall almost egg-shaped thing with a queer tufted piece perched atop it. Curly realised the buildings and beyond must belong to the Pineapple, and he now knew where the ranch had gotten its queer name.

The grey-blue pall of the sky was lightening; it became gradually pink, then the sun broke shyly through. Its rays burnished the queer shaped rock, making it look more like a pineapple than ever. As he rode to it Curly gazed upwards but the reflected rays of the sun made him blink. He lowered his head, pulled his hat-brim over his eyes.

It was a sudden jerk of his horse's head which warned him. He looked swiftly at the ground in front of them, suspecting a rattlesnake. Then his hat was whisked from his head; with the flat boom of the shot, he let himself fall from his horse and was rolling as soon as he hit the ground.

He jerked upwards to his knees and, squinting, reached for his gun.

'Don't be silly, pardner,' said a cool sardonic voice.

Everybody called everybody else pardner, it seemed, in this neck of the woods. He saw the man on the rocks above him with the gun glinting in his hand, and the other man moving up behind him. He took his hand away from his gun and got to his feet. His pony stood trembling a few yards in front.

The second man passed the one with the gun and began to descend the rocks. Curly bent to pick up his hat.

'Leave it!'

The cowboy straightened quickly: there was no mistaking the menace in that voice. The second man reached level ground and advanced. He was taller than Curly and thinner – and had a yellowish horse-like face. He swayed forward on his high-heeled boots and his one hand was on his gun. His eyes were pale and rather shifty.

In his turn Curly watched, one eye on the man above. The tall fellow came nearer.

'Take his gun, Hank,' said the other. 'Ask him what he's doin' here.'

'All right,' snarled the yellow-faced man out of the corner of his mouth. 'I know! I ain't deaf an' dumb – or simple.'

The pale shifty eyes widened a little as he came nearer. Here was a gink you could trust no more'n a diamond-backed sidewinder. Curly watched the wide-awake hat Hank wore, saw the man above blotted out by it for a second and moved.

The slug kicked the dust up in front of his toes, the echoes of the gun rolled in his ears: the look-out had moved too.

He called down: 'You aimin' to die young, pardner? Don't do that again.'

Curly shrugged, smiled crookedly. The pale eyes in front of him looked a little sick now. The horse-faced man had his gun half out of his holster. He let it drop.

Curly knew he could have beaten him if the marksman up there hadn't put in his oar once more. He could have beaten him easily! And *he* certainly did not claim to be fast on the draw.

The man's horse-like face seemed a little yellower. He sidled away from Curly's look. Here was a back-stabbing skunk if ever there was one – and no more guts than a spavined jack-rabbit.

Hank drew his gun as he moved to Curly's side. He said softly: 'Don't make any more funny moves or I'll let you have it.'

'I ain't scared o' you, beany,' Curly just as softly.

18

'But I don't want a slug in the guts from your pard up there.'

He saw the vicious light in the pale eyes, the sudden movement, and he ducked. The swinging gun brushed the cloth of his shirt at the shoulder.

'Drop it, Hank,' said the man above. 'I nearly plugged you then. Keep still, yuh damned fool.'

Hank took Curly's gun. He said nothing but his yellow face had gone suddenly lined and his pale eyes spoke murder.

'Get away from him,' said the man up top.

Hank turned his head. 'I don't hafta take orders from you, Grinewold.'

The other man, with the dark, smooth face, sardonic like his voice, did not reply to this. His lips quirked a little at the corners and he began to descend the rocks. His hat was pushed well back and the sun burnished the blackness of his hair at the temples.

Hank was silent, trying to watch both of them at once, as if he was the transgressor now, unfriendly to both of them.

Grinewold reached firmer ground. As he advanced Curly realised now he had him in the right perspective, he was a little smaller than average, but perfectly modelled, well-dressed – for a cowhand. The little half-smile remained on his lips as he said: 'You're trespassin' on land belonging to the Pineapple Ranch, pardner. What's your business here?'

'You Pineapple men?'

'Obviously.'

19

'Do you always shoot at people who happen to wander across your holding?'

'Invariably.' The voice was mocking. It went on: 'Now *you* answer some questions, stranger. Be good – it's your turn.'

Curly did not immediately reply. This was a queer set-up. He had worked for smaller spreads – no fences – open land, neighbourliness. But he had heard that some of these big cattle barons in other parts of the West were crazily jealous of their holdings. Still, what harm could a lone saddle-tramp like him do? He was curious – but easy: he decided to play along. He said: 'I'm lookin' for a job as a cowhand. This is cow-country, ain't it – this is the big spread?'

'This is the big spread all right. Where'd yuh come from?'

'Just the other side of the border. The Ringo country.'

'I know it. Small stuff.'

'Yeh, small. But good.'

'Who'd yuh work for?'

'The Crooked Wheel, Jeb Cannock's place. An' further south before that – the Alamo.'

'What made you move here?'

Curly shrugged. 'Nothin' to hold me. Figured I'd find me some new mountains.'

'Somep'n to hold you if you stopped mebbe. Somethin' with bars.'

'They hadn't a saloon back there with a bar that good.'

20

'I didn't mean them kind of bars.'

'I figured you didn't.' Then Curly shook his head. 'Whadyuh want: a cowhand, or a saint on hoss back?'

'I ain't even said we want a cowhand. You'd hafta see Bill Crowe about that.'

Who's Bill Crowe?'

'The ranch-manager.'

'Ain't you the ranch-manager?'

'Nope.'

'For a galoot who ain't ranch-manager you ask a helluva lot of questions.'

'He's gettin' lippy, Dave,' snarled Hank suddenly. 'Let's work him over then send him back where he comes from.'

Dave – 'Grinewold' no longer now that Hank's bile had simmered down – did not answer. Then he said: 'We can't do that, Hank. I guess we'd better take him in.' Dave turned to Curly. 'Git up on your hoss, pardner.'

The cowboy mounted the paint, gentling the little beast with his hands and with clucking sounds of his tongue.

Hank reappeared from behind the rocks, leading two horses. The Pineapple men mounted.

'Ride jest in front, pardner,' said Dave. 'An' remember, all the time, what a good shot I am. Head for the ranch at a trot.'

'That's where I was making for anyway,' said Curly. He grinned pugnaciously. 'I certainly hope that Bill Crowe hombre sets me on – maybe I'll get a chance to even up with you two gents.'

'Maybe you will,' said Dave. There was a chuckle in his voice: he did not sound alarmed at the prospect. Hank said nothing: Curly could almost feel the murderous glance boring into his back.

As they got nearer to the ranch a bunch of riders passed them.

'What yuh got there?' yelled one.

'A new fish,' replied Dave Grinewold. 'We're gonna find out whether we've got to keep it – or throw it back.'

The men laughed. They were a tough-looking bunch.

Curly admired the layout as he rode closer to it. The main buildings consisted of three long one-storey log cabins and a two-storey frame house painted white and with a wide verandah running around it. This latter Curly figured was the ranch-house; and a right handsome place it was too. There were the usual barns, outhouses and haystacks spreading like a rash on all sides of the main buildings.

Dave ordered Curly to dismount outside a small frame hut which stood on piles. Four steps led up to the narrow door. On this latter was inscribed largely, in a glaring white paint, the word 'Office'.

'My, my,' said Curly. 'Real classy.'

'Not so much lip,' snarled Hank. He had his gun out once more.

'Put *that* away,' said Dave.

Hank scowled but did as he was told.

'You can get back to the look-out,' the other told him.

Hank's scowl became ferocious, his pale eyes were shifty.

'I don't hafta take orders from you, Grinewold,' he said for the second time that morning.

Oh, f'r Pete's sake – what in hell's the matter with you? Would you like to see Bill Crowe an' let me mosey along?'

'All right,' mumbled Hank. He turned his horse's head with a vicious jerk.

Dave watched him as he rode away. He almost seemed to have forgotten Curly. They were alone, there was nobody else in sight except the rapidly-diminishing figure of the man and horse. If Curly wanted to jump the dark dapper man now was his chance. He did not take it.

Dave's expression was sardonic as finally he turned towards the cowboy. Curly echoed his thoughts.

'Objectionable sort of a gink that Hank.'

'Yeh.'

'He's got my gun.'

'You'll get it back I guess.'

'I certainly hope so.' There was an edge to Curly's usually good-natured voice. 'I'm mighty attached to that gun.'

'A man gets that way,' said Dave carelessly. He climbed the four steps and rapped on the office door.

A voice said, 'Come in.'

Dave looked back at Curly. He seemed to be debating with himself. Then he said, 'Wait there, pardner,' opened the door and passed through it, leaving it a little ajar behind him.

Curly heard the murmur of voices but could not distinguish any words. He looked about him.

A figure came out on to the white verandah of the ranch-house. It was just a flicker of movement which made Curly turn his eyes fully in that direction. At first he could not see the figure plainly, for it was white, the same colour as the trim fretted bars behind which it stood. Then Curly saw the face and the body above the bars and realised it was a girl who stood there, was turning her head and beginning to look in his direction.

He could not see her very clearly from where he stood but it seemed like she was pretty. The sunshine glinted on her reddish-gold curls making them a burnished and glittering halo. She wore a white shirt-waist with a red brooch, or maybe a rose, pinned to the breast. Her arms were bare and she leaned there on the rail of the verandah and looked at Curly.

He doffed his hat and she inclined her head gravely. He did not think she smiled at all: she reminded him of an English duchess he had once seen when he had taken a trip back East with Jeb Connock when the old man was putting through a big beef deal.

Curly had not liked the big city; the dudes, and the painted women who made him sick. He did not like the way the population turned out to gawp at this fat painted sprig of British nobility as if she was some-thing great and abnormal. He contrasted her with the girl on the verandah, who looked so fresh and sweet, windblown. She was turning away now. She did not look in his direction again. He had a last flashing white glimpse of her before she disappeared into the house. He was left with a sense of exhilaration, coupled with a faint puzzlement. He was no longer 'easy', there was a tense waiting, almost hoping, about him. The feeling was not unpleasant.

He found himself hoping that he would get the job he sought. It seemed very important that he should. There was so much he wanted to find out about this mysterious place.

CHAPTER THREE

He started as the door above him was opened widely.

'Come on in,' said Dave Grinewold.

Curly climbed the steps and entered the office. Dave let him pass and closed the door behind him.

Curly found himself confronting a big hunch-shouldered man who sat at a small table, strewn with papers, before the window.

Smouldering eyes looked up at him out of a granite-like face, all the features of which seemed to be above normal. The nose was jutting and misshapen, as if a great hand had pulled it then twisted it. The brow was like the upturned lip of a cliff, with vegetation growing on the edge of it – thick bushy greying hair, tufted eyebrows. The mouth was a wide stretched line, the cheekbones high and jutting; the chin came out almost as far as the nose and was deeply cleft. The man's face was clean-shaven. It was granite-like – coloured that way too.

The deep-set smouldering eyes looked Curly up and down. He bore their scrutiny with equanimity.

He was doing a mite of weighing up himself, noting the man's faultlessly cut broadcloth, bulging at the shoulders and the upper arms with the power of the body inside it, the snow-white linen and shiny black silk cravat, the grey silk waistcoat with the dainty pink fleur-de-lis and white pearl buttons.

Looking closely at Bill Crowe. Curly figured he was well past middle age but hard-wearing and well-preserved and with as much respect in himself and vanity in his own appearance as the young man, the sardonic Dave Grinewold.

He realised suddenly that Crowe was speaking to him.

'I guess you'll know me when you see me again, young fellah.' His voice was a bossy rasp.

'Guess I will,' said Curly.

The big man grunted. Then he turned to Dave.

'Go find Hobel – he's around here some place. Tell him to come right away. Then you can go back to your job.'

'Yes suh,' said Dave Grinewold and left the office with alacrity.

Bill Crowe looked at Curly again. 'Take off your hat, young fellah,' he said.

The cowboy obeyed the order mechanically. Then he grinned.

'Sorry, suh,' he said.

He was weighing the big man up once more and saw that he was a little mollified. His voice was not so harsh, but it still had that bossy ring, as he said: 'Where'd you come from?'

'I've already told your hand all that.'

'Tell me.'

Curly told him. The big man said: 'You've got it all word perfect, haven't you?'

'It's the truth.'

'And you're not on the run?'

'Nope. I wouldn't come to a big spread like this if I was, would I?'

'You were coming here when the boys picked you up.'

'Yes, I was.'

'Who told you to come here?'

'Nobody in particular. I jest heard there was a big ranch outside town. I liked the country. I figured I'd like to stay here a while—'

'We expect our men to stay some time – if they're good enough. If they're not they're pretty soon told about it. Then if they don't mend their ways they're given their time. Once you're booted from the Pineapple you're finished as a cowhand in this territory. Our men have got to be good.'

'That's straight.'

'Can you ride, shoot, rope—?'

'Ever since I was knee-high to a grasshopper—'

Somebody rapped on the door and Crowe called, 'Come in.'

The door opened. The man stooped under the lintel as he came in. He was about six foot six and a regular beanpole. His small head was perched atop a scrawny neck and narrow sloping shoulders. The face was wizened and brown, like a walnut, but the eyes were young and the corn-coloured hair had no hint of grey.

'You sent for me, Mistuh Crowe?' he said.

His voice seemed to come up from his boots and gather a lot of gravel on the way.

Bill Crowe said: 'Yes, Sam. I've got a new man for you. What did you say your name was young fellah? Speak up.'

Curly was a little nonplussed by the sudden realisation that he had been hired. He forgot to take umbrage at the boss's tone. He blurted out, 'The name's Joe Simpson. Everybody calls me Curly.'

'This is Sam Hobel, the foreman.'

The two men shook hands and eyed each other. They both said, 'Howdy.'

'Take him out, Sam, and show him the regular ropes.' Maybe it was just imagination but it seemed to Curly that Crowe stressed that 'regular'.

Sam Hobel opened the door and went down the steps. As Curly began to follow him Crowe said: 'Wait a minute.'

Hobel halted on the steps. Curly turned at the door.

Crowe said: 'You do as Sam Hobel says and ask no questions. We don't like people who try to run things for themselves. We're a team – we like to work like one: the boys have got a rough way with anybody who don't. You'll get along with them I guess.'

He turned to his desk, picked up a paper.

'Come on,' said Sam Hobel. A little puzzled, Curly followed him. As they crossed the yard, leading his horse to the stables, he said: 'Who's the big boss here – the owner?'

Hobel squinted down at him. 'I'll tell you all you gotta know,' he said. 'Then quit it. You're here to work not ask questions.'

'I'll work,' said Curly. 'But I'm no dog – don't talk to me as if I was, mistuh.'

'If you're gonna work for me I'll talk to you how I damn-well please.'

An angry retort rose to Curly's lips but he choked it back as Hobel went on. He was answering questions: he certainly was a queer gink. Maybe he didn't mean to be offensive.

'The Pineapple belongs to a combine. Bill Crowe's the manager – as far as we're concerned he's the big boss. And believe me, he knows his job. You don't play fancy with Bill Crowe.'

Curly was on the point of asking the name of the combine but he checked himself. He had an idea Hobel wouldn't tell him anyway. So instead he said: 'Does Crowe hang out here?'

'He lives at the ranch-house … Anythin' else you'd like to know?' There was no change in the gravel-like voice. Curly was not sure whether the foreman was being sarcastic or not.

The inevitable question bubbled to his lips but he kept them tight. He'd find out who the girl was later. When he spoke he merely said: 'How about pay? He didn't tell me what the pay was.'

'The pay's good. You want the job don't yuh?'

'Yeh.'

'All right. There are the stables. Gimpy'll take care o' your hoss.' Hobel raised his voice. 'Gimpy! Where the hell are yuh?'

From the shadows in back of the stables a bent limping figure appeared, a little old man with snow-white hair. He came out into the light and Curly saw his face, and the illusion of gentle old age was dispelled by the look of the wrinkled grimy visage upon which was imprinted evil, as plain as the brand on a steer's flank.

Gimpy stopped walking and Curly saw that his one leg was shorter than the other and the foot small, like the foot of an eight-year-old boy.

'Whadyuh want, Sam?' The voice was cracked and whining.

'Take care o' this man's hoss. He's new.'

'I ain't expectin' hosses this time o' day. They're all out.'

'You'll look after this one. Take him. Feed him an' rub him down.'

Curly collected his bedroll and his saddle. Then Gimpy took the horse.

'Take good care o' him,' said Curly.

Gimpy did not answer. He gave Curly a vicious glance then he led the paint back into the gloom. The little cayuse seemed to follow him quite willingly.

As they walked towards the bunkhouse Sam Hobel said: 'Don't worry about your hoss, Gimpy 'ull take care o' him. He thinks more o' hosses than he does people – on account of that leg o' his I guess.'

Despite his looks, his manner, his grating dominating voice, Curly figured Hobel was a sensible sort of fellow. Anyway, he wouldn't be ramrod of a big spread like this if he hadn't got something in that narrow head and beanpole frame of his. He would be a handy man to have in a pinch. He needed watching … Why did he think he *ought* to watch a member of the Pineapple? Curly thought: maybe it was because there was an aura of mystery around the place. and that was engendered by a disgruntled ex-employee – Carrots.

Had anything happened to bear out Carrots' air of 'something not quite right somewhere'?

He had been shot at. Yeh – but he had the sense to realise that Dave Grinewold, being a marksman, had only done what he intended to: shoot his hat off. If things had gotten really ugly would he have shot to kill, Curly wondered There was no telling with that cool, dressed-up little cuss..

Then there was Hank – he was bad, if ever anybody was. Still there was usually one of his kind on every ranch.

There was Bill Crowe's reception of Curly. But he had set him on hadn't he? Quickly too. His questions and remarks had been very enigmatic. Still, maybe Curly would not have thought them so were it not for the way things had gone in town.

And there was Sam Hobel. It was a little difficult to try and judge Sam Hobel while his unusual presence was so close. He was looming over Curly now as he opened the door of the bunkhouse and ushered him inside. Although the foreman was so much taller than the new man it was doubtful whether he was any heavier.

Curly looked around the long low room with the bunks all round the walls, except at the two windows, the large scrubbed table in the centre, the two pot-bellied stoves, the chairs and benches strewn across the cleared expanse of bare floor.

It was a good bunkhouse, but rather chilly, un-homely. Still, maybe that was because it was empty. No, he was wrong, it wasn't empty! On a bunk against the opposite wall lay a man.

Just then Hobel's voice rasped in Curly's ear. It was louder, it made the cowboy start.

'Kruger! Damn you, Kruger – get up!'

The man on the bunk stirred and groaned.

'Kruger!' said Hobel again. He crossed the room in three long strides, grasped the man's shoulders and shook him.

The man moaned again, then said thickly, 'Leggo o' me. Whassamarrer wi' yuh. Leggo. I'm sick I tell yuh. Leggo.'

'You're drunk,' grated Hobel. 'Get off that bunk.'

The man rolled over and turned his face to the wall.

Hobel seemed to lose all patience suddenly. His long body bent. He grabbed the man with both hands and dragged him violently from the bunk.

Kruger rolled along the floor and hit a leg of the table. He grabbed it and began to haul himself slowly to his feet.

'I'm sick,' he kept mumbling. 'I tell yuh I'm sick.'

The two men watched, Hobel one side of the table, Curly the other. Kruger worked his way upwards slowly until he was leaning across the table. He faced Curly and finally his bleary eyes became fixed on the new man.

'Who's this?' he said. 'Who's this? Whadyuh want here, uh? Whadyuh want?'

He began to work his way slowly around the table and Curly realised he was indeed drunk – or at least suffering from the great grandaddy of all hangovers. He was 'sick' all right. Sick-drunk!

He reached the corner of the table. He was almost facing Curly. Hobel behind him, stood watching motionless, no trace of expression on his face. Without warning Kruger launched himself forward.

Before Curly could get out of the way the man had crashed into his legs. Curly toppled, the door jamb held him up. The door was half-open.

Curly tried to wriggle his legs free, thinking the man had paid himself out, would let go. But Kruger held on like a leech and suddenly heaved himself upwards. Over his head Curly saw the expressionless face of Hobel, then Kruger clawed up at him like an animal. A sharp nail raked Curly's chin. Drunk or no drunk, he was not standing for that – he hit out. His fist connected with Kruger's ear. The man's body bent backwards but he held on, trying to pull Curly over with him.

'Let go, you crazy loon!'

Kruger's only answer was a slobbering curse and

another raking movement with his hand. Curly jerked his head sideways and the set of long nails narrowly missed him. Kruger was only holding on with one hand: Curly hit him hard in the stomach.

Kruger let go. He fell at Curly's feet and writhed with pain.

'Serve him damn well right,' said Sam Hobel.

'What's the matter with him: is he kinda touched?'

'Not ordinarily. He jest gets that way when he's drunk. I've never seen him quite this bad before. He must have taken a dislike to yuh – mebbe he thinks you're a pink elephant, you being new.'

Curly looked in puzzlement at Hobel. There was no hint of levity in the foreman's face, in the tone of his voice.

Kruger began to rise again. He was pitiful now, moaning, his face gleaming with sweat.

'Boot him outside,' said Hobel.

Curly hesitated. Hobel noticed his hesitation and came round the table.

CHAPTER FOUR

Kruger was half-stooping. He turned towards Hobel. 'Sam,' he said.

That was as far as he got: Hobel pounced on him, grabbed him by the scruff of the neck, spun him towards the door. Then he kicked him. There was a calculated brutality about it all which rather sickened Curly. The long lean figure, the little head, the expressionless face, the swinging boot, the sickening thud as the toe of it struck Kruger's flesh with vicious force. Curly half-started forward, then cursed himself and stopped. Was he going to stick his neck out for a drunk he didn't know? and one who had attacked him too.

He was suddenly sorry for his own brutal retaliation. But at least it had been hot-blooded, not cold and vicious like Hobel's.

He followed the thin man to the door. Hobel stepped outside, facing his man.

Kruger rose to his hands and knees. Tears were streaming down his puffed, bleary-eyed face. He was a pitiful sight. But in Curly's pity was mixed a contempt. He suddenly wanted to grab hold of the man and slap him and shake him. He understood a little how Hobel had felt. *Or did he?*

'I didn't mean any harm, Sam. Honest. I didn't like the way he looked at me, that's all. Who is he, Sam? Who is he?'

'He's the man who's gonna take your place.'

'Take my place?' Kruger echoed the words like a child, as if they were meaningless to him.

'I told you to get out of here with the rest, didn't I?'

'I was sick, Sam.'

'You were drunk. This is the last time. I never rode you when you came in from town night after night drunk. But now it's interfering with your work. You're no good. You're jest a damn' sot. You're finished, Kruger—'

'Finished.' Kruger echoed this word. Then his eyes focused on Curly and he went back to his old note. 'Take my place,' he said. 'Take my place.' His voice rose to an almost-scream. He tried to get to his feet and dive forward, all in one movement, and he fell flat on his face. A queer sound broke from Hobel. It sounded like a chuckle. But when Curly turned his head he saw nothing there.

Kruger rose to his knees once more.

'Get your stuff an' get off the place,' said Hobel. 'You can get your money the end o' the month. Write for it – or call if you're still around. I hope you ain't. Go on – get going!'

Kruger seemed to have forgotten all about Curly. He rose to his feet quite easily, mechanically. Tears streamed down his face once more.

'Going?' he said. 'Sam – I bin here seven years. I bin here longer'n you, Sam.'

'That's just it,' rapped Hobel. 'You've bin here longer than me so you think you can get away with anythin'. Get your stuff an' get off here pronto – unless you want me to have you rode out on a rail …'

Kruger's tears stopped suddenly. He became surprisingly sober too.

'You wouldn't do that, Sam. Not to me.'

'I will if you don't make yourself scarce – pronto!' Hobel shot these words out, his voice getting higher. Then he turned on his heels.

'Come on,' he said.

Curly looked at Kruger, who was standing with his head hanging, then he followed the foreman back into the bunkhouse.

Hobel waited until he was inside then slammed the door behind him. There was no petulance about the gesture, just a deadly finality. Truly, Sam Hobel was a man to be reckoned with.

He acted now as if nothing had happened. He said: 'You might as well take that bunk. You'll get fresh blankets for tonight.'

He pointed to the one Kruger had vacated. Curly spoke before he had given himself time to think.

'I didn't figure on taking another man's job off him.'

'You ain't,' said Hobel. 'Kruger was for the high

jump anyway. You'll take that bunk.'

The door behind them was opened. They both turned their heads. Kruger came in.

'What do you want?' said Hobel.

Kruger's face was set, lined. He looked older. Middle-aged. He said: 'I jet came back for my gun-belt an' my 'makings'.'

'Get 'em.'

Kruger passed the two men: he tottered a little, crossed to the bunk with the tumbled clothes. From under the pillow he took the little wash-leather sack which contained his 'makings'. Then he delved down the side of the bunk, against the wall.

Finally he brought forth a well-worn greasy belt with a shapeless holster containing a walnut-handled gun. He was half turned away from the two men as he buckled the cartridge-belt around his waist. He was slow and fumbly.

'Don't take all day,' said Hobel. 'Get out of here. Get going!'

Kruger whirled. His gun was in his hand. 'If you say that again, Sam, I'll kill you.'

His gun was pointed at Hobel, but the barrel was slanted downwards.

Curly saw the foreman's face tighten. Then he was looking at Kruger again.

'Don't be a fool,' said Hobel. His voice was softer than Curly had heard it yet.

Kruger's bleary eyes were suddenly shifty, they glared but they could not focus.

'Get out,' said Hobel softly.

'Sam,' screamed Kruger. It was as if he was driving himself to shoot.

Hobel moved suddenly, his body bending. Smoke wreathed his hip. Kruger was falling as the gun crashed, its report deafening the enclosed space. Kruger was falling and his face was crumpling, his eyes staring, appealingly. As if he wanted Hobel to stop this thing that was happening to him. But Hobel did not move. His gun was still at his hip, its muzzle pointed at Kruger, blue smoke still curling from it. And Kruger's gun was slipping from his lax hand and Kruger pitched forward suddenly and fell on top of it.

'Sam,' he said. It was just a choked whisper. Then his face was pressed flat to the bare boards and he was still. From beneath him a thin line of blood began to run sluggishly.

The terrible suddenness of the thing temporarily paralysed Curly. He could not realise what was happening: Kruger had fallen down again. Then he saw the blood and he knew. Next moment he had drawn his own gun and was covering Hobel.

The foreman turned. His gun was still at his hip, now its muzzle was pointed at Curly. The two men, death in their hands, faced each other.

'What did you want me to do?' said Hobel. 'Let him shoot us to ribbons?'

He turned away from Curly, holstering his gun at the same time. He bent over Kruger and rolled him over. 'He's dead,' he said.

Curly admired the man's guts. His rage had

subsided and he felt almost sheepish.

'He was drunk,' he said.

'Drunkards often shoot straight,' said Hobel. He straightened, listening. 'Put your gun away, there's somebody coming.'

Curly heard the footsteps too. He shrugged, but there was no nonchalance in the gesture this time: it was forced. He sheathed his gun.

The door burst open and Bill Crowe came in.

'What's going on here?' he said.

Then he stopped dead in front of the table. His surprised face became moulded once more into its hard craggy lines as he looked down at Kruger. He looked at Hobel.

'Is he dead?' he said.

'He's dead all right.'

'What happened?'

'He was skulking in here. I turned him out. He got nasty and pulled his gun. I had to shoot him. Simpson here saw it all.'

'That right, Simpson?'

'He was drunk,' said Curly.

'Yeh, he was drunk,' said Hobel. 'But he had a gun in his hand. He might've killed us both.'

'That right, Simpson?' said Crowe again.

'Yeh, I guess so. He might not have pressed the trigger – an' then he might've.'

'You don't seem sure. You'd better get your story right for the law.'

Crowe added, with seeming irrelevance: 'You're a Pineapple man now you know.'

'Yeh,' said Curly. The addition seemed relevant to him. 'I guess Kruger asked for it. He took an awful chance an' it blew up in his face.'

'Get him on to a blanket,' said Crowe. 'Cover him up. I'll send Gimpy for a couple of the boys and you can take him into town.'

'Hadn't we better leave him here and send for the sheriff?'

'I don't want that fat slob crawling around here like a snuffling pig. Do as I say.'

'Yes, suh,' said Hobel. 'Come on, Simpson.'

He crossed the room, grabbed a blanket from off one of the bunks. As he turned he almost cannoned into Curly who, obeying orders, had followed him.

'What yuh doing – tracking me?'

'Changed yuh tune haven't yuh, mistuh?' said Curly.

The foreman did not say anything. But Curly saw his eyes and they were not pleasant. He thrust the blanket into the new man's hands.

'Lay that out beside him.'

Curly took it. Crowe stood by the door and watched as the new man smoothed out the blanket by the side of the body. Hobel joined him and said: 'Now roll him over on to his back, on to the blanket.'

They rolled Kruger over, his wide appealing eyes looked up at them, the face crumpled like that of a crying child's. Curly felt a sudden sadness, a crushing sense of frustration. If he'd had his wits about him maybe he could have prevented this. The man had been unknown to him, had been a drunk and a crazy

43

coot. In his drunkenness he had wished the new man harm. But, even so, the easy-going Curly could not have wished this upon him.

With a flick of his wrist Hobel sent the blanket over the body, covering the face completely. There was no more Kruger. Curly had not known him – he must forget him.

'Wrap him up,' said Bill Crowe in a deep toneless voice.

Then he turned as the door behind him was opened. Curly looked up. The girl stood there.

'I heard shooting,' she said in a breathless voce.

Her eyes were wide, dark – maybe dark blue. Her hair, now he saw it clearly, was a bright corn-colour. There was her shirtwaist, and the red brooch, the full high breasts, the long brown skirt, little red moccasins on her feet.

She gasped and with her gasp Bill Crowe's voice boomed harshly.

'Teresa. What are you doing here? I've told you over and over—'

'The shots.' The girl's voice was suddenly deeper, in it there was something of the man's harshness. She moved then, looked past him as if to see better the blanket-shrouded form.

Her fist went up to her mouth, small white teeth on her knuckles. Then her eyes met Curly's. She connected him with everything and in her eyes was a sudden loathing. Then she turned as Bill Crowe spoke again.

'This is no place for you, Teresa. The bunkhouse is

never the place for you. Get back to the house.'

'That man. He's—'

'He's dead.'

The girl turned swiftly and Curly did not see her face again. The door closed behind her.

'What are you staring for, Simpson?' said Crowe. 'Get on with your job.'

'Catch hold,' said Hobel.

Curly bent mechanically. He was not easily riled. Anyway, right now he was thinking about the girl. He helped the tall ramrod lift the mummy-like form.

'Put him in a corner out of the way,' said Crowe.

They carried the body into a corner behind one of the unlit stoves and placed it down there.

'Clear up the mess, Simpson,' said Crowe.

Mechanically Curly looked at the place where the body had been. There was a wide stain, a spidery trail. He looked up at the ranch-manager. He forgot all about the girl, Teresa. He said: 'You hired me as a cowhand not an undertaker's mop-lady.'

Crowe looked back at him. 'All right, Simpson,' he said. Then he turned on his heels and opened the door. 'Get your horses,' he called over his shoulder.

The two men stood relaxed for a moment. Curly looked at Hobel. The foreman said: 'I was waiting to hear whether you'd say yes or no to him. Either way he was likely to kick you off the place. He don't like having his orders disobeyed – but he don't like folks with no guts either. If you'd done what he asked he'd've figured you were gutless. An' then, if he had kept you on, boy, your life wouldn't've been worth living around here. Like he told yuh: we have some tough boys. An' their boss is the toughest of the lot.'

'We live an' learn,' said Curly.

He followed Hobel as the tall man strode for the door. They went through. As they crossed the yard, Crowe was leaving the stables. Without a glance in their direction he turned and walked towards the house.

Gimpy came out of the stables and ran, with curious hopping steps, towards them.

'I guess he didn't hear the shots at all,' said Hobel. 'He's kind of deaf.'

Gimpy stopped. He said: 'The boss says I got to ride out pronto an' fetch a couple of the boys. What's up?'

'You do as you're told,' said Hobel. 'Get back in there and fork your nag. If you're not back in fifteen minutes with two men I'll skin you alive.'

Gimpy's eyes flashed a look of hate. Then he turned back. He hopped in front of them.

Hobel said softly, 'Gimpy was kind of attached to Kruger. Almost as if he was a hoss. I don't want an argument with the cantankerous old goat right now.'

Curly looked up into the foreman's face. It wore no expression of cynicism.

When they reached the stables, Gimpy was already leading out a small pony. Curly noted that one stirrup leather was much shorter than the other. The old man mounted and without a word, urged his horse to a gallop. He sat easily in the saddle – he was a good horseman – and his bent back made him look like some kind of gnome, with white shining hair curling from beneath his battered Stetson.

Curly and the foreman got their horses ready. Hobel was silent now. Curly figured his recent confident manner was just a flash in the pan. To test this he hazarded a question.

'Who was the girl?'

'I ain't here to answer your questions. You'll find out sooner or later I guess. Keep your tongue away from her – an' your eyes, too.'

'I just wondered.'

'You wonder a damn' sight too much.'

Curly felt a sudden spasm of irritation.

'If I was to pull up stakes and burn the wind from this territory you'd lose your witness, wouldn't you, mistuh?'

'Don't do that, pardner!'

CHAPTER FIVE

It was noon when Curly, Hobel and the other two men rode into Ramrod city. One of the men led another horse with the blanket-shrouded body of Kruger lashed to the saddle.

People passing by looked at them covertly, their mouths dropping open at the sight of the bundle. Loungers on the boardwalk stared and turned to chatter.

Into the doorway of the livery-stables came Carrots, Curly's early-morning friend. His cross-eyes did not seem to be looking at anything in particular but he nodded slightly in the cowboy's direction. Curly nodded back and out of the corner of his eye saw Hobel watching him. Carrots disappeared into the gloom of the stables.

A few seconds later the cavalcade halted outside a box-like frame building, with an equally box-like adobe structure tagged on to the side of it. The wall of the latter was black – except where small boys and wags had chalked and scratched messages upon it. Messages and words like 'Board and Lodging free',

'Calaboose', 'Hotel Cooler', 'Hoosegow', which left no doubt in the reader's mind as to what kind of building this was. Two windows with dirty net curtains shielding them looked out from the other building and there was a narrow weather-beaten door on which was inscribed in faded white paint the words, 'Sheriff's Office'.

The four men dismounted and hitched their horses in a bunch to the short tie-rail. Why so many men to bring one dead body into town, Curly wondered. Was it because the imposing ramrod of the Pineapple had to have a retinue when he rode into town. And particularly maybe when he brought trouble like he brought it now. The two cowhands were hard-looking characters who looked like they could handle any other trouble that was likely to happen along.

They unlashed the body from the horse, one took the head, the other the feet, and they carried it across the boardwalk. The foremost one let go with one hand and lifted the latch of the office door. Then he kicked the door open. A fat man in a big hat was on the point of coming out. He started back, his mouth formed a small black 'O' in his fat red face.

Curly lost sight of him as he moved to let the two men and their burden pass. Then the cowboy followed Hobel into the office. He closed the door behind him.

The two men placed the body on a bench against the wall. One of them sat at its feet, holding the shrouded legs with one hand to prevent the bundle from rolling off. His pard stood in front of the bench, his thumbs hooked, with a curiously aggressive pose, into his belt.

The fat man stood against the desk and looked at the bundle and from one to the other of the four men. His eyes finally rested on Hobel and stayed there.

'What's this?' he said. His voice as high and squeaky and breathless.

Hobel jerked a thumb at the bundle on the bench. 'That's Ike Kruger,' he said. 'We had an argument this morning and he pulled his gun. I had to plug him. This young fellah's my witness. Kruger was crazy – if I hadn't've shot when I did he might've got us both. He attacked this young fellah first of all then he turned on me.'

'Drunk?' said the sheriff. 'He was always drunk.'

'He was drunk,' said Hobel. 'But he knew what he was doing all right.'

'He was crazy drunk,' said Curly.

'He pulled a gun like Mr Hobel said?' the sheriff queried.

'Sure.'

'And he meant to shoot?'

'It looked that way.'

'An' Mr Hobel was justified in killing him?'

'He was justified in shooting him. I'm sorry he killed him.'

'Do you think it was justifiable homicide or not, young fellah? Answer yes or no.'

Curly could not say the actual homicide had been

necessary, but the shooting had, and when shooting was going on anybody was liable to get killed. It might have been him. He could not truthfully say 'no' to the question. These thoughts flitted rapidly through his mind the split second before he spoke.

He answered, 'Yes.'

The sheriff turned away and rolled across the room to the body. Curly suddenly remembered what Bill Crowe had called him. 'A fat slob'.

Although that could have been a description of the sheriff it was certainly not a kind one. It had been spoken in contempt. Yet Curly found nothing in the sheriff to be actually contemptuous about. He was slow maybe, lazy, but he was certainly shrewd enough.

He said to the Pineapple man at the foot of the body, 'Move over, son.'

The man scowled and moved. With thick clumsy fingers the sheriff moved aside a fold of the blanket and looked down at the body.

'A straight shot through the chest,' he said. 'He didn't live long after that.'

'He died almost instantly,' said Hobel.

The sheriff turned again and pushed his big hat back from his forehead with a thick forefinger. His eyes, pouched in fat, were penetrating as they looked at Curly.

'You're new here, ain't yuh, son?'

'Yeh, just rode in this morning.'

'What for?'

'Looking for a job.'

'He came out to the Pineapple first thing,' said

Hobel. 'Bill Crowe gave him a job.'

The sheriff turned his gaze from Curly and looked at Hobel.

'What did you an' Kruger quarrel about? Had it anything to do with this young fellah?'

'Wal, in a way, yes.' Hobel told the story. He told it pretty straight.

When he had finished the sheriff nodded his head ponderously. He looked at Curly.

'How do you tell it, son?'

'Just like that.'

The sheriff nodded again. Then he went off at a tangent.

'Where'd you come from, son?'

'Everybody asks me that,' said Curly. 'I never saw such an inquisitive burg.' He told it again, all of it.

The sheriff kept nodding and writing down things on a little pad on his desk. As Curly finished talking the door behind him opened and another man came in. He was little and wiry and he wore his gun very low-slung. His dark face went truculent as he saw the company.

'Oh, Branch,' said the sheriff. 'Nip down the street an' tell Craddock he's wanted, pronto, an' he'd better bring his boy along.'

The deputy's eyes found the figure on the bench. He scowled at the Pineapple men who stood nearby it.

'Yes,' he said. The door banged behind him.

The sheriff straightened himself. He looked at Curly. 'You may have to give evidence, young fellah, you may not. It seems a straight case.' He turned to

Hobel. 'By rights you should have left things as they were and sent for me – you know that. Tell Bill Crowe I'm coming out to the ranch this afternoon to look things over.'

'He figured that wouldn't be needed if we came to you.'

'Maybe not. Maybe I'll come, maybe I won't. Tell him I might anyway.'

Curly saw Hobel's face tighten. But the lean foreman did not say anything but, 'Come on boys.'

The three men followed him out. As they untethered their horses, Branch, the deputy, came along the boardwalk with two other persons in tow. One was a tall fellow in black, the other a freckle-faced kid who by contrast wore a brilliant red shirt.

'The undertaker and his boy,' said Hobel.

As the four of them rode along the street, leading the riderless horse, Curly said: 'I'd better go get my war-bag. It's at Tiny's place. I owe him some time, too.'

'Owe him some time?'

'Yeh.' Curly turned his horse's head.

Hobel said: 'Be at the ranch this afternoon. I'll leave Klaus with you.' He jerked a thumb.

The blue-jowled puncher with the bristly moustache turned his horse and joined Curly. Hobel and the other man, with the latter leading the riderless horse, continued down the street.

Curly said nothing. Klaus was beside him as he hitched his horse outside Tiny's rooming-house. Klaus jerked a thumb. He said: 'I'm going down tuh

54

the saloon. Don't be long.'

An angry retort rose to Curly's lips. Then he checked it. Klaus was already swaggering down the boardwalk. He was heavily built and looked in fighting trim. What was the use anyway, thought Curly. Klaus had his orders.

Curly went into the rooming-house. There was nobody in the lobby. He crossed it and opened the door at the back. There were already plenty of diners in the lunch-room. Curly looked around the room then over towards the kitchen. After a moment he saw Tiny and Tiny saw him. He nodded his head and came over. Curly backed into the lobby. When Tiny came through shutting the door behind him, shutting out the noise, Curly said: 'I've got a job. So if you'll lead me to that little chore I was promised I'll do it, then get my war-bag an' go. Sorry I ain't stayin' with you longer. Thanks for everything anyway.' He grinned. 'Lead me to them dishes.'

'Forget it, pardner,' said Tiny. 'You've bin straight with me. You ain't no dishwasher. You can pay me any time.'

Curly had half-expected this. He grinned again. 'Thanks pardner,' he said.

Something like a smile wrinkled Tiny's fat round white face. 'Go get your war-bag, pardner,' he said. 'I've got to go upstairs. I'll come with you.'

Neither of them spoke until they reached the room. Tiny was puffing a little. He stood in the doorway while Curly crossed the room, picked up his war-bag, turned with it in his hand. Then the fat man said: 'So you've got a job, uh? Quick work. Outside town?'

Curly chose his words quickly, watched the fat man to note his reactions to them. 'Yeh. The Pineapple.'

The expression in Tiny's little black eyes did not seem to change. But Curly thought he saw a subtle change in the flabby face. It did not look so genial. But maybe that was just his imagination. Tiny merely grunted and said: 'You got your cowhand's job then?'

'Yeh,' said Curly. He went back across the room. Tiny stepped aside to let him pass then, after closing the door, fell into step with him.

He dropped behind Curly as the cowboy descended the stairs. At the bottom Curly turned and said: 'I thought you wanted somep'n from up there.'

'Did I? Yeh, so I did. Wal, never mind. I'll get it later.' Tiny held out his hand.

'So-long, pardner.'

Curly caught hold of the huge flabby paw, velvety at first then powerful as it gripped his fingers.

'Adios, amigo.'

'It'll be long adios, pardner,' said Tiny as he let go of his hand.

Curly looked at him, puzzled. Tiny went on: 'You seem to me like a reasonable sort of young fellah. I don't like telling yuh what I've got to tell yuh.'

'What's that?'

'As long as you work for the Pineapple you ain't welcome in my place. I don't want to see you in my place again. Don't ask me why, I don't want to get ornery. Just shake your pins an' get out of here.'

Curly saw the little black eyes glinting, he choked down the questions which clustered on his tongue.

'All right, Tiny,' he said. He turned abruptly and left the place.

After the gloom of the lobby the rays of the sun struck him in the face like a physical blow. He squinted; almost winced. He was suddenly furiously angry. Not at Tiny, not at anybody in particular, unless maybe it was himself. And why he should be angry at himself he could not explain. A man had got to live, hadn't he? He'd got to do what seemed best to himself. He could always change his mind – but a man who kept changing his mind got nowhere, fast. Ever since he got to this burg folks had been trying to tell him what to do, or trying to influence him in subtle ways. What was the matter with these people? Were they jealous of the Pineapple and its rich lands? Or was there a deeper meaning? Had he hired out to the Pineapple or hadn't he? He had! Right; then if it was anybody's right to give him orders it was the right of Sam Hobel and Bill Crowe – and certainly not the right of any tinpot townsman!

He was striding out, hardly looking where he was going, forgetting his horse at the tie-rail, when he almost barged into a man who appeared suddenly in front of him. It was the little squint-eyed fellow, Carrots.

Curly was truculent but when Carrots said, 'Howdy, feller,' and grinned his snaggle-toothed grin the cowboy's truculence died. He was not made that way: and besides there was something about the little runt he could not help liking.

He said, 'Howdy.'

Carrots fell into step beside him. 'Goin' to get a drink?' he said.

'Yeh, I guess so. Comin'?'

'Sure.' Carrots pointed. 'Brodie's is the best.'

He was silent then. Curly held his peace, waiting for the next. Finally it came.

'So you got yourself fixed up then?'

'Yeh.'

'I saw you comin' in.'

'Yeh, I know. I saw you.'

'Got business for the sheriff, uh?'

'Yeh, somebody got shot.'

'Looked like he got shot purty bad – if'n that was him in the blanket.'

'It was. He was dead.'

'Who was it?'

'A man named Kruger.'

CHAPTER SIX

'Kruger!' There was a new note in Carrots' voice. He stopped walking.

Curly stopped, too, almost automatically. He looked at Carrots. The little lean man's squint-eyes were wide, there was hurt in them.

'Who did it?' he said softly.

'Hobel.'

'That buzzard!' Carrots spat out the words savagely. For a moment his blackened gappy teeth looked like fangs.

Instinctively Curly found himself defending Hobel almost as if he was defending himself.

'I was there. Kruger drew first. He was crazy drunk. He might've killed both of us if Hobel hadn't got him first—'

'Kruger was allus drunk. He was a fool. He got worse – all the time he got worse, I think I know why he got worse.' Carrots' talk was savage, fast, garbled. He was suddenly a different man. 'But he wasn't a real bad guy. He wouldn't kill anybody. I've seen him pull a gun before when he was like that. I've seen him fire it into the air. I've seen him point it at people, but then he never pressed the trigger. He wouldn't. Everybody knew that. Hobel knew it. He knew it I tell yuh.'

His words were sinking into Curly's mind, beginning to stir uneasily there. He said softly, choosing his words carefully, 'Was Kruger a friend o' yourn, Carrots?'

'I rode with him a lot if that's what you mean. You don't make friends at the Pineapple.'

'What do *you* mean?'

'Nothin' I guess. Jest nothin'.' Carrots was talking softly now, sullenly. He began to walk again, Curly beside him. He continued to talk.

'Why did Hobel shot Kruger?'

'I told you why Hobel shot him. Listen.' Curly told him the old tale again. It did not make him impatient to have to repeat it once more. It was as if he wanted to get it all straight in his own mind. As he talked he suddenly realised that fat Tiny had not said anything about the cavalcade, the blanket-shrouded form, the visit to the sheriff. Maybe it hadn't reached Tiny's ears yet. That was curious, him keeping a place like he did. Maybe he had heard, maybe that was why he had told Curly to keep out – though he had said that applied to all Pineapple men. Why did it apply to all Pineapple men .... Curly was all mixed up in his mind. He was talking mechanically.

Carrots heard him out then he said, 'An' you were the only witness?'

'Yeh.'

'An' you told the sheriff Hobel was justified in killing Kruger?'

Curly admired Carrots' perceptive powers. He said: 'I couldn't tell him anythin' else.'

'Did the sheriff believe yuh? He knew Kruger too.'

'It was the truth. What the hell are yuh gettin' at?'

'Nothin',' said Carrots. 'Nothin'. I ain't callin' yuh a liar if that's what you mean. There's just different ways o' lookin' at things that's all. You bein' a stranger, look at things one way, you can only look at things one way: other folks might look at 'em another.'

'You're a reg'lar little riddle-me-ree feller, ain't you?' said Curly. He had regained his sense of humour, had temporarily placated his unruly mind.

Carrots did not say anything to this. His sudden spasm of temper seemed to have exhausted him. The two of them passed through the doors of Brodie's saloon and made for the bar. Klaus was already there. Curly was a little surprised, he had temporarily forgotten about the man. He had an idea that Carrots hesitated a little in his stride when he saw the other Pineapple man. However, he carried on and they bellied up to the bar; Curly next to Klaus, Carrots beside Curly.

The latter said 'Howdy' but Klaus did not answer. He looked at Curly, then he looked past him, at Carrots. He looked hard, there was a scowl on his blue-jowled face.

Finally he said: 'I ain't drinkin' with him.'

If Carrots heard the words he gave no sign. Curly said, 'You ain't drinkin' with him, uh? Why?'

'Bill Crowe don't like his men drinkin' with town fish. Particularly town fish who useter belong to the Pineapple.'

That savage irritation creased Curly's mind again. He said, 'So Bill Crowe don't like that, uh? An' what Bill Crowe don't like his lapdogs don't like either.'

'Hey,' said Klaus. 'I—'

Curly, the bit between his teeth, went on unheeding. 'Carrots is drinkin' with me whether you an' Bill Crowe like it or not. I was gonna ask you to drink, too, just like you seemed to take for granted! but you can please yourself an' to hell with yuh—'

'That's strong talk. I don't—'

'You don't, uh. You're full o' don'ts ain't uh? Wal, get your don'ts to hell away from me an' drink some place else.' This was what he had been boiling up to. He was enjoying it. He was sick of folks trying to tell him what to do.

Carrots grabbed his arm, interrupting his flow of words. 'Tain't no use havin' a lot o' trouble. I know when I ain't wanted. I cain't say I'm keen to drink with Klaus either. I'll mosey along.'

He moved but Curly had hold of him, a vice-like grip on his wrist.

'You ain't drinking with Klaus. You're drinkin' with me like you planned. You're stayin' right here. It's about time I told you people what to do for a change—' Curly was concentrating on Carrots. He was half-turned away from Klaus but out of the corner of his eye he saw the man's sudden movement and he swung round, swerving a little at the same time.

Klaus's fist struck him on the shoulder, rocking him on his heels. His back hit the bar. Klaus's follow-up blow missed him entirely. He saw Carrots snarl, his hands moving downwards: he flung himself side-ways, grabbed the little man's wrist.

'Back,' he said. 'I'll handle this.' He spun Carrots away from him. He turned swiftly.

Klaus's hand came away from his belt. He lashed out. Curly ducked, bored in, head down. He drove two hard punches into the other man's body. Klaus was tough: he staggered back, doubled a little then, just as Curly figured he was wearing him down, swung a vicious uppercut to the new man's jaw. It straightened Curly up, knocked his head back. Klaus bored in, throwing punches from all angles, driving Curly before him.

Chairs crashed over as men got quickly out of the way. They began to form a rough ring around the combatants. The barman pleaded in vain for 'Order'.

A smashing blow to the side of his head sent Curly down, his side against the brass foot-rail beneath the bar. He rose slowly, shaking his head, watching Klaus warily from beneath lowered brows. He realised he was up against a seasoned brawler. He might even have bitten off more than he could chew. Out of the corner of his eye he saw Carrots watching him anxiously. Then he launched himself upwards, both fists moving out like pistons. They landed on Klaus's heavy face, sending sweet shocks to Curly's elbows. It was the other man's turn now to give ground.

He hit the bar with his back, then launched himself from it like a stone from a catapult. The two men clashed in the cleared space, slugging, the blows smacking and thudding.

Curly was driven back into the crowd, rallied, and as Klaus came on too eagerly, stopped him with a punch in the middle, straightened him up with two more blows to the face. But the man seemed made of teak. He shook the blows away, drove on through Curly's guard. The crowd had Curly again. They pushed him back hard. There was a roar of laughter as the two men missed each other.

As Curly stopped himself with his hands on the bar-top he heard somebody shout: 'Come an' have a look at this. Two Pineapple men fighting each others.'

He turned with his back to the bar. He faced Klaus, who stood with his chest heaving, his arms crooked, held forward, waiting.

Then another, high voice rang out. 'What's goin' on here? Let me through!'

Klaus turned as the fat man broke the ranks behind him. It was the sheriff and he had a gun in his fist.

Klaus backed, nearer to Curly, who leaned against the bar and remained still. The sheriff looked from one to the other. His eyes were shadowed beneath his big wide-brimmed hat. The gun was held laxly in his hand, pointing in their general direction and some-where about the region of their thighs. Neither of the two men seemed inclined to test the sheriff's marksmanship.

He said: 'Don't tell me you two ginks 've been fighting. I thought you were out o' town long since.'

Somebody in the crowd sniggered. Klaus said sullenly, 'We had some chores to do.' He seemed deflated.

The sheriff said: 'Wal – wal, I never expected to see a couple of Pineapple men fighting each other.'

There was that phrase again: that irritating phrase. And the sheriff was looking at Curly and continuing with his spiel.

'Trouble certainly sticks to you, young fellah. I should advise you to ride right on outa town an' don't come back till you've simmered down or you're due for some time in the cooler.'

Before Curly could speak Klaus said: 'Jest a little private squabble, sheriff. Nothin' bad. It's all finished now. C'mon, Curly.'

Curly was stubborn. 'I'll have my drink with Carrots first. Then I'll come.'

Klaus shrugged. 'Suit yourself.' He turned and bored his way through the crowd.

Carrots came forward diffidently and stood beside Curly. They turned to the bar. Curly ordered drinks from the open-mouthed bartender. He felt somebody beside him and he turned. It was the sheriff. The fat man said: 'What was the fight about, young fellah?'

Curly said: 'I'm sick of answering questions.'

65

Carrots chimed in. He told the sheriff the truth. The sheriff made a sage remark.

'You can't play both aces at once, son. One of 'em's likely to turn out not to be an ace after all.'

'Everybody here talks in riddles,' said Curly.

The sheriff said, 'I'll buy you a drink. Then I think you'd better leave town an' keep out for a spell.'

'I—'

Carrots interrupted quickly. 'Better do as he says, Curly. Look around yuh.'

Half-unconsciously Curly had been becoming increasingly aware of the ominous buzz behind him. Now he turned. The townsfolk were clustering nearer, looking at him, with far from friendly eyes. He heard the name 'Pineapple' mentioned more than once.

He was suddenly very weary. He was just a hard-working cowhand: he didn't want any trouble.

'All right,' he said. He turned back to the bar. The sheriff shoved a drink towards him. He said 'Thanks' and took it.

He drained it in a gulp. 'I'll be seein' yuh,' he said.

Carrots gripped his arm then let it go. 'All right, feller,' he said. The sheriff said nothing. Curly realised suddenly that he did not even know the fat man's name. Yet the impact of his personality on the young man had been quite forcible.

He left both of them. The crowd parted to let him through. As he passed through the doors of Brodie's place he heard somebody say 'Killer'. Whether the word had anything to do with him or not he did not know. He did not care.

CHAPTER SEVEN

He walked back to the tie-rail outside Tiny's place and mounted his pony. He sent the little beast at a walk past the saloon. They weren't going to hurry him.

Carrots came through the door. He looked surprised to see Curly only just passing there. He raised his hand in salute. Curly tipped his hat in acknowledgement then he set the paint at a canter.

As he rode on to the trail he saw a rider in front of him. He guessed it was Klaus, it looked like his blocky figure.

Curly did not slacken his pace and, as he got nearer, the man turned in his saddle and looked back. It was Klaus all right. He reined in his mount. Curly did not know what to expect as he approached him.

Klaus did not say anything. He looked out front once more and set his mount at an even pace beside Curly's.

They rode in silence for a few moments before

Klaus finally spoke.

'We'll hafta tell Bill Crowe about that ruckus. Get it in before somebody else does. He's got his spies in town.'

'Why in hell should he have spies?'

'He jest does. He'll be hoppin' mad if he hears about things from somebody else. We'll tell him that we just had a difference of opinion an' there wasn't no harm in it.'

'Was there?'

'Naw, I guess not. That Carrots gink gets in my craw. No guts. I was surprised to see yuh come in with him in tow that's all.'

'You forget I'm a stranger hereabouts. You can't expect me to know all the Pineapple prejudices – or abide by them. I had breakfast with Carrots before I rode to the ranch. He seemed a nice little gink to me. A kind friendly sort of a gink.'

'No guts,' said Klaus again. 'Forget him.'

'Get one thing straight, pard,' said Curly. 'I'll drink with Carrots any time I like as long as he's all right with me.'

Klaus shrugged. 'Suit yourself. I'm not your boss. It's just that, like I told yuh, Crowe don't like us hobnobbing with the town boys. No offence.'

'No offence,' said Curly. He held out his hand.

Klaus turned his head to look at him then he grasped the extended hand. Curly could not tell by his expression whether the gesture was genuine or not.

They carried on again in silence for a time then

Klaus said, 'I'm kinda sorry about Kruger. He wasn't a bad galoot. But he's bin askin' for it a long while, waving his gun about when he had them drunken fits of his. I guess Hobel wanted to get rid of him.'

'That wasn't no reason to kill him.'

'I didn't mean it that way.' After that Klaus shut up like a clam.

They hit the trail to the Pineapple.

Klaus was silent. Curly was thinking.

He was thinking that he needn't stay at the Pineapple if he didn't want to. He could pick up his bedroll and carry on riding, forget all about the ranch, and Ramrod City, and whatever went on between the two places. Whatever it was that went on between them he could not yet figure out .... Hell, he did not have to figure it out. He could leave the whole damn' boiling behind him.

All of a sudden he realised that if he did ride on while the Kruger case was still hot from the fire the sheriff would want to know the reason why, and might even send a posse out after him. He did not want the law on his heels: he liked to travel in a leisurely fashion. He reckoned he'd better stay till all that had blown over. Bill Crowe had said he liked his men to stay. Maybe that was one way of making them do so, making them acknowledged Pineapple men: embroiling them in a ruckus like the shooting of Kruger. Hobel had made him witness, maybe he would have to give evidence. If he did, that would stamp him a dyed-in-the wool Pineapple man.

He knew without telling that he would not be

popular in town. It irritated him that he did not know why. By what he had seen of both townsfolk and Pineapple folks there wasn't much to choose between them. He almost wished he had not stopped in this territory. But he knew curiosity – and the sheriff – would hold him there for a while.

He thought again about that sheriff and on the heels of his thoughts said to Klaus, 'That fat lawman ain't as dumb as I expected him to be.'

'What made you think he was dumb?'

'Oh, the way Bill Crowe spoke about him this morning I guess. Called him a fat slob, said he didn't want him snooping around the ranch.'

'Yeh, Bill Crowe would say that I guess. But Gus Emmett ain't dumb, no sirree.'

'Gus Emmett?' echoed Curly. It was the first time he had heard the sheriff's name yet the sound of it struck a chord in his mind. It jangled for a while – then he remembered.

''Not Gus Emmett, of El Paso?' he said.

'The same.'

'I'd heard he was dead.'

'Wal, he ain't. He settled here a couple years ago. The townsfolk elected him sheriff, they figured his reputation 'ud scare the hard cases away I guess.'

Curly thought to himself that maybe Klaus was one 'hard case' who had not been scared.

The dark, blocky man with the little bristle moustache went on talking.

'He's got fatter an' fatter. I guess he ain't half the man he useter be.' Klaus chuckled. 'In another way

70

he's double the man he used to be.'

Curly tittered at the obvious joke. He figured he would play along with the man for a while – at least as long as he was feeling communicative.

'After the way Bill Crowe spoke about him I was expecting any fat, lazy tinpot lawman. I certainly didn't expect it to be the man who tamed some o' the worst hellholes o' the West.'

'He's fat an' he's lazy – but he still ain't no tinpot. It's said that him an' Bill Crowe knew each other in the old days – but how or when nobody seems to know. They hate each other like pizen. They've had squabbles over the men an' different things in town—' Klaus paused. Then he said, 'Aw, it ain't no skin off our noses I guess,' and he shut up altogether.

Curly waited a bit. Then he said: 'Everybody knows a lot about Gus Emmett. He's famous. Some o' the tales ain't true I guess – but many of them are. Yet I never heard mention of a Bill Crowe in connection with him—'

'Nobody knows much about Bill Crowe. And it ain't wise to ask questions anyway – he's a mighty powerful man.' Then again Klaus shut up.

Curly let things go. He did not want the man to turn nasty again. But he could not help thinking about Gus Emmett; if he delved down into his mind he could recall so many tales about that almost legendary figure. There was nothing, however, to tell him why Emmett should choose to settle down in Ramrod City. Maybe he just wanted peace .... Was he getting it?

And Bill Crowe? Where did he fit in? Why did he hate Gus Emmett? Was Bill Crowe his real name?

Curly realised he could go on asking himself questions – and getting no answers. He was making mysteries out of nothing. He'd better quit it before he scared himself half to death.

They were approaching the cluster of rocks, the chief of which gave the ranch its queer name. Klaus said: 'Gosh, I shore am lookin' forward to some chow.'

Up on the 'pineapple' rock they saw Dave Grinewold and the hatchet-faced Hank. The former waved and the two cowboys waved back. But Hank gave no sign.

Curly began to think about the two men. The one, despite the fact that he had taken a shot at him, he did not dislike. The other he could quite cheerfully hate. A snake if ever there was one, that Hank. What was his story? Hell, did everybody have to have a story? Hank was just a humdrum cowhand like himself.

He forgot Hank and looked about him, looked towards the ranch-house. He, too, could do with some chow. His thoughts then became the thoughts of any humdrum cowhand: what was the chuck like at this particular spread?

He was looking at the bunkhouse when the horse and rider came into his line of vision, swerving, coming towards them. The rider was a slim form; sun glinting on golden hair. The girl Teresa. She swerved her mount again as if to avoid them.

72

'The Crowe gel,' said Klaus. 'Out for her after-lunch canter. She's still got that damned hoss I see, the headstrong young hussy.'

Evidently the cowhand did not approve of Teresa Crowe or her nice-looking white stallion. Curly said: 'What's wrong?'

'That hoss ain't bin broken but a week. Sam Hobel told her he wasn't safe to ride. But she's bin out on him a coupla times an' he ain't thrown her so I guess she thinks she's top dog.'

'She certainly knows how to ride.'

'She does that,' said Klaus grudgingly. Then he added: 'An' she knows it.'

The girl passed, a distance away from them, and did not look in their direction.

'She ain't so high-falutin' as she pretends to be,' said Klaus. 'It's just that maybe her uncle might be watching her.'

'Uncle? I figured him for her father.'

'Naw. She calls him Uncle. Same name. I guess she's his brother's child. I ain't seen – or heard about any other kith or kin of either of 'em—' Again Klaus shut up suddenly as if he thought he was talking too much.

Curly did not say anything. He was sick of hearing about the mysterious Bill Crowe. As he turned to look after the girl he did not give a damn if her uncle was watching him with the aid of binoculars. He admired her trim figure in the short tightly belted leather jacket, the firm shoulders, the long glossy hair streaming from beneath the brown 'bowler'.

His eyes became fixed as the set of the shoulders suddenly seemed to waver. He realised that the white stallion had slowed down but was prancing awkwardly.

The girl was jerking at the reins. Curly saw the horse's neck arch, the head twist viciously as the beast tried to snap its rider. The girl raised her quirt and lashed him across the flanks. Curly could sense the rage behind the movement. That young lady liked to have her own way. But, with a beast like that one, she wasn't using the proper method to gain obedience. The horse revealed that fact in no uncertain way. He began to buck viciously.

Curly stopped his own horse, holding his breath as he saw the girl leave the saddle. But she regained it again. She was a fine horsewoman. Her body was taut, her knees clasped to the horse's flanks. Curly did not think she was strong enough, she would get thrown eventually. What that horse needed was a bronc-buster, he wanted 'breaking' all over again.

He heard Klaus say, 'What's bitin' you?' then he was urging his mount forward.

Whether Klaus was following him or not he did not know. The little paint raced like the wind which whistled in his ears. The hooves thundered and all the time the stallion was doing new tricks and the girl was hanging on like grim death. All the time she was sagging a little more, being thrown from side to side.

The horse came down, all four feet at once; his whole frame quivered. Then it bounded forward, neck stretched and started on a mad gallop.

Curly had seen killer stallions in breakneck headlong flight before. They often finished by smashing
themselves and their rider. He was deadly afraid as he
coaxed the last ounce of speed out of his gallant little
cayuse. But all the time he knew the cow-pony could
not emulate the lightning run of the stallion, could
not hope to lessen the distance, let alone catch up.

The girl was hanging on, leaning forward flat over
the horse's neck. As long as she kept that way and the
horse continued to race she was pretty safe. If the
horse did not stumble in his headlong flight: pictures
flashed through Curly's mind, he had seen just that
happen once, the horse pitch, the rider thrown over
its head and trampled to death beneath the flying
hooves.

He felt sickening horror. Such a thing must not be
allowed to happen to that beautiful girl!

There were other alternatives: the horse could
run until he was spent and trembling and his rider
could dismount unhurt. Or he could stop suddenly
and roll, pinning the rider beneath him. Or he
could buck, taking the rider by surprise and, in her
now weakened state, throw her easily. Or he could
find some obstacle on which to smash himself, a
suicidal madness which often overtook a proud half-
broken beast like that one. What a fool the man had
been to let her ride him. What a fool she had been
to do so.

Images, hopes, curses flashed through Curly's
mind, escaped from his tight lips, all mixed up in the
medley of thudding hooves, rushing wind, the sight

75

of the racing figure in front; and the never-diminishing space between them.

They were approaching the rocks now and from their shelter rode Dave and Hank. They cut across to intercept the racing stallion. Dave was in front, his black head bare, glinting in the sun. He had his sombrero in his hand and slapped his horse's flanks with it from time to time.

The white horse saw them and, hardly pausing in its stride, swerved away from them. Curly saw his chance and aimed at doing a bit of intercepting himself. The horse, probably terror-stricken at the sudden appearance of Dave and Hank, did not see him.

He was running erratically now and the girl was jerking in the saddle. She turned her head towards Curly, her face white and strained; her eyes staring. She was at the end of her tether.

The paint pony bored in from the side, getting nearer every second. Curly made a reassuring gesture to the girl but it was doubtful whether she saw it. Curly was scared she might suddenly tumble from the speeding horse through sheer inability to hang on any longer. Her grip was trance-like: he must be careful not to do anything which might cause her to break it.

As he cut across at right angles to the stallion's flight the distance between them was lessening. It seemed that the horse had not yet noticed the newcomer. Curly was afraid of what might happen when he did. He thought he saw signs of weariness in the racing beast, an almost imperceptible uncer-

76

tainty in his stride. He checked his own horse's pace a little, keeping the regular short distance between them now, biding his time.

The girl turned her head once more. She seemed to see the man then, even to recognise him. He admired her guts as a little strained smile crossed her face.

He made a reassuring gesture and formed sound-less words with his lips. 'Hold on, honey. Hold on.' The 'honey' part slipped out unconsciously and whether she was aware of it or not he could not tell.

Then the thing happened which Curly had feared. The horse saw him and with terrible suddenness stopped and reared at the sudden apparition, this added terror. Even as a scream bubbled to Curly's lips and died there the girl was falling. Her feet left the stirrups and she was free. She hit the ground and lay still. The horse pranced and snorted, its eyes rolling.

Curly screamed at it, took off his hat and waved at it as the paint bounded forward. The stallion backed away from the advancing sight, away from the still form on the ground, then turned and raced on.

Curly leapt from the saddle and went down on his knees beside the girl. He bent his head closer to her and she stirred. He put his arms gently round her shoulders but did not lift her, fearful of what might have happened.

'Miss Teresa,' he said and the voice did not sound like his own.

She tried to get up, her eyelids fluttering. There was no pain in her face. He increased the pressure at her shoulders and lifted her slowly. She sat up.

Next moment her arms were around him and her face was buried in his shoulder and the strain poured from her in great gulping sobs.

He held her and he could feel the softness of her, could smell the perfume of her hair, could feel the desperate strength of her as she clung to him. He patted her shoulders and made little inarticulate reassuring noises and she clung to him tighter. Then Dave and Hank and Klaus arrived and clustered around them and he looked and she let him go. She quit sobbing and would not look at him as he helped her to her feet.

CHAPTER EIGHT

Teresa had been put to bed by the housekeeper, the white stallion had been roped and was standing docilely in a corner of the corral and Klaus and Curly were standing in front of Bill Crowe in his office.

The big boss had thanked the four men, and Curly in particular, for saving his niece. He was not lavish in his praise and was louder in his censure of 'that fool girl'. She had been inarticulate, and even seemed a little cowed, as she was taken away. Her thanks to Curly had been mere mumble and, in the presence of the others all the time, she still would not meet his eye.

Curly wanted no favour for his act and he was pretty sure, judging by the boss's attitude, that he would not receive any. That business was already finished with, Curly let it go too and strove to forget about the girl, though the feel of her, the scent of her, still stayed with him, dazing him a little.

Bill Crowe was looking at him keenly. Then he turned his gaze to Klaus.

'Have you two been in a fight?' he said.

'We had a little difference of opinion, suh, an' came to blows. No harm – didn't mean nothing.'

'You mean to say you fought each other?' Crowe's voice was louder, harsher.

'Wal, yeh, but—'

'Where?'

'In Brodie's place.'

Crowe's granite-face went pink. 'In Brodie's place. Among a herd of townsfolk I guess.' He repeated himself for emphasis. 'Two Pineapple men fighting in Brodie's in front of a herd of townsfolk! And you say there was no harm, it was nothing! What was the fight about?'

Klaus hesitated so Curly chimed in without pausing to think first.

'Klaus objected to my drinking with a certain townsman.'

'What townsman was this?'

It was Curly's turn to hesitate: he wished he had not opened his mouth.

'It was Carrots,' said Klaus.

'Carrots! That whining, narrow-gutted little coyote!'

Angry words rose to Curly's lips but he choked them back. He was getting good at bottling things up lately. Crowe turned to him and said: 'What do you know about Carrots?'

'I met him at Tiny's when I had a meal. I thought he was a friendly little cuss.'

'He used to work for me.' Curly did not divulge

80

the fact that he already knew that and the big boss went on: 'I kicked him off the place because he was no good He's doing some lickspittling job in town now and he hates the Pineapple like poison. We don't hate him, we despise him. No wonder Klaus objected to your association with him. He's gutless and he's got a mean, lying tongue. You'll find all that out in time I guess. I don't want to have to keep telling you these things. I want you to understand that there are certain unwritten rules by which Pineapple men have to abide. The main one is that what I say goes or – through me – what Sam Hobel says. One of the things I don't like is my men hobnobbing with the townsfolk. Y'understand?'

'Klaus has already told me about that. I'm learnin' fast.'

Crowe went on as if the cowboy had not spoken. 'My men have good pay, good chuck. Conditions are the best. In return for this I expect them to do as they're told, and no questions asked. Y'understand?'

This time Curly said nothing. He merely nodded. Even so he was surprised at his own tame acquiescence. He wanted to stay at the Pineapple a while: he knew that! Why? Was it maybe because of that girl, Teresa? Was he getting jelly-legged over a woman? The thought was novel, sobering.

He started a little as Bill Crowe said: 'All right, get going, both of you. Sam Hobel will give you your orders right after chow.'

The two men left the office silently and crossed the yard to the mess-hut, which was the long log-building to the right of the bunkhouse, connected to it by a lean-to and a side door.

Men were leaving the place and going to the stables. Most of them spoke to Klaus; some of them to Curly, but many just gave them hard glances. He noticed anew what a tough-looking bunch they were. But they had a competent look about them which was often lacking in the happy-go-lucky staffs of smaller spreads. They were better dressed; and all of them seemed to have sat down to chow still wearing their gun-belts, their low-slung guns.

Curly and Klaus took their seats among the debris and dirty plates of the rapidly emptying tables. A greasy-faced man in a yellow apron stuck his head through the kitchen door and said: 'Late ain't yuh?'

'Shut the lip an' let us have some chow, pronto,' retorted Klaus viciously. 'An' let it be good an' hot an' fresh.'

'Awlright,' said the man. They could hear him grumbling to himself as he withdrew his head. Klaus produced a packet of store-cigarettes and took one. He pushed them along to Curly.

'No thanks. I'll have one after the meal.'

Klaus shrugged and pocketed them. He lit up, leaned back, and blew smoke rings. Curly could sense the hard arrogance of the man. The whole atmosphere of this spread was like that; arrogant – flaunting its arrogance.

The yellow aproned man came in with the chow, two steaming plates of it on a tray. A pudgy kid followed him with mugs of coffee.

'Thanks,' said Klaus. He gave them a cigarette apiece.

The two cowboys set to ravenously. Curly had to admit the excellence of the chuck – and the flapjacks and molasses, and the hot, greasy doughnuts which followed it. This was washed down with another mug of sweet, thick coffee and Curly was ready for one of Klaus's cigarettes.

They were sitting back smoking luxuriously when the door opened and Sam Hobel snaked his way in. He stood on the threshold with his back slightly bent and peered at them.

'When your lordships are ready—'

'Comin', Sam,' said Klaus, and jumped to his feet. He dropped his half-smoked cigarette and ground it beneath his feet.

Curly rose more leisurely and, still smoking, followed Klaus to the door. Hobel turned and led them out. Then he swung around. His cold eyes bored into Curly's face.

'Put out that weed,' he said.

Curly shrugged and snubbed out the glowing end. Then he put the half cigarette into the pocket of his leather vest.

'Get your hosses,' said Hobel. 'Then fetch the wire-repairing tackle. There's a hole in the fence by the corner water-hole. Fix it. That ought take yuh the rest of this afternoon – an' no longer.'

'All right, Sam,' said Klaus. 'Come on, Curly.'

They got their horses then rode to the tool shed which was at a corner of the corral. From the other side of the fence the white stallion rolled a liquid eye at them. There was no sign in him now of the 'killer' of an hour or so previous. Seeing him reminded Curly once more of the girl. He wondered whether she had gotten over her shock, whether she was thinking of him.

Hell, why would she be thinking of a common cowhand like himself?

'Catch,' said Klaus and in the nick of time he threw up his hand and clumsily caught the huge wrench the man tossed him. He cursed as it knocked his thumb up.

'You'd better look alive, Curly,' said Klaus. 'Or you'll be bawled at for daydreaming.' As he was dragging out a bale of wire he said reflectively: 'I remember once we had a guy here we useter call "Bugs". He was kinda weak in the head I guess an' a proper woolgatherer. Bill Crowe loosed off a gun behind him an' scared him half to death.'

'A ripe sense of humour Crowe's got,' said Curly.

He wondered what his reactions would be if the big boss let off a gun behind him. He caught deftly the wire-cutters Klaus tossed him; caught them by their handles, not by their cruel, shining blades. He thought, irrelevantly, what a handy weapon those twin-pointed blades would make.

He put the cutters into the long pocket of his leather chaps and the wrench into his saddle-bag. Then he helped Klaus hang the bale over his saddle horn. A bag of staples and a hammer completed the collection and they set out.

'I didn't figure a big spread like the Pineapple 'ud need fences,' said Curly. 'There ain't no adjoining spreads are there?'

'No, not what you'd call spreads. There's a few nesters. They ain't welcome.' Klaus chuckled. 'They come an' go purty quickly .... There's only that one stretch o' wire.'

He pointed. 'Up there by the ridge – you'll see it purty soon.'

The 'ridge' was an outcrop of low rocky hills which broke the flat skyline for about half a mile.

Another fifteen minutes riding brought the two men to their base and Curly saw the thin three-strand fence.

'The break'll be this way I guess,' said Klaus, jerking his horse's head around.

The hills were L-shaped, their flattest part being the corner of the letter. In this corner was a small water-hole. They found the break in the fence behind the water-hole. They dismounted there and, looking through a gap in that rock-strewn part of the small range, Curly could see the plains behind. They were arid, rocky, scrub-ridden – in direct contrast to the lush land behind him. The dying late-afternoon sun threw a red glow over the scene, giving it a strange other-world appearance. No living thing moved over this table-like blood-tinted expanse.

Klaus said: 'Would you believe it that settlers try to farm that land!'

Curly did not answer right off. Finally he said: 'I'd believe anything of settlers. They're a breed different to the normal run. They've got more guts than the average. My folks were of that breed. They didn't amount to much in the end but there was somep'n about 'em I guess.'

'They're dead?' said Klaus. It was half a question, half a statement, and spoken in a perfectly flat voice.

'Yeh, they're dead,' said Curly. He looked up, through the gap once more, out across the arid plain. 'Any settlers there now?'

'I don't think so. Leastways, if there's any new ones I ain't heard about it yet …. You daydreaming again, Curly? Here, gimme a hand with this wire.'

'Sorry, Al,' said Curly. He had only recently learnt, through the folks speaking to Klaus at the mess-hut, that the man's first name was Al. He did not seem to bear any malice after the fight. He seemed a reasonable sort of a fellow, though a hard case and one who would bear watching closely if things went wrong between them again.

As he strained, helping the strong blocky man with the bale of wire, Curly wondered what could go wrong. Was he troubling himself with mysteries once more? He stopped pondering and concentrated on the job in hand.

They carted the stuff to the edge of the fence and inspected the damage. A couple of stout wooden posts had been uprooted and the wire was in a twisted mass.

'What could have done that?' said Curly.

Klaus did not offer an opinion. All he said was, 'Best thing we can do is snip the ends o' this, tie a rope to it and get one o' the hosses to drag it away.'

Curly hesitated. Then he said: 'You cut the wire an' I'll go get my cayuse.'

He turned. The horses were browsing beside the water-hole. As he approached them Klaus's nag went down to the edge and lowered his head to drink. His nose was almost in the water when he shied away, snorting irritably.

Curly was puzzled as the horse turned away and began to crop grass. He went down to the edge of the water-hole and looked into it. The water was still and a little muddy. Curly was about to get down on his knees and taste it when he checked himself. If Klaus's horse did not like it maybe he wouldn't either. He turned to his own little paint, got hold of his bridle and led him to the water.

'Where's that hoss an' rope?' bawled Klaus. 'What in hell are yuh playing at?'

Curly did not answer his pardner. Instead he spoke gently to the paint, and stroked his neck. The little best lowered his head to drink. He paused with his nose a few inches above the water. His nostrils quivered.

'What's the matter, ol' feller?' said Curly.

The horse backed away, looking at the water, then rolling his eyes upwards to his master.

Klaus strode behind them. 'What in tarnation's the matter with yuh, Curly?'

Curly said: 'There's somep'n the matter with that water. The nags won't drink it.'

'It's all right,' said Klaus. 'Just a little sour. The

cattle drink it all right.' He went down on his knees before the water, made a cup with his hands and dipped them. He bent his head and took a drink.

He spat it out quickly and cursed. He rose to his feet, shaking his wet hands.

'Gosh, it does taste kinda queer,' he said. His scornful attitude had changed suddenly to one of alarm and suspicion. It was a quick about-face, hardly too violent to be due solely to the nasty taste of water.

'Bill Crowe 'ull have to know about this.'

As Klaus finished speaking his face changed suddenly, a horrible look of surprise came over it. Then it began to contort in agony as he clutched his stomach and doubled up.

CHAPTER NINE

Curly caught him as he pitched forward. He was still writhing as he dragged him to a patch of grass but his movements were becoming weaker. He was merely twitching as Curly laid him on the grass.

There was a line of white foam on his open lips and his tongue protruded. His eyes rolled, showing the whites horribly. He tried to say something and his words made a jerky croaking sound. Curly bent nearer.

'*My stomach* … it's burning … It's all over me … Water—'

Curly ran and fetched his water-canteen. When he returned Klaus was lying still. His eyes were closed and his breath was coming in jerking gasps. His face was yellow and shiny with sweat. His mouth began to work and more white froth bubbled from between his lips.

Curly uncorked the canteen and tilted it gently to Klaus's mouth. The lips shut like a trap as if the man's jaws had been suddenly locked. The water ran down his chin. He became still and his breathing was suddenly inaudible.

Curly corked the canteen and dropped it quickly beside him. He bent and placed his head to Klaus's chest. His heart was still beating, but very faintly.

Curly bent and worked his arms beneath Klaus's body. He grunted as he lifted. The man carried a lot of weight and he hung limply as if he was already dead. Curly placed him across the front of his own saddle then mounted up behind him.

He called Klaus's horse and, with it speeding behind him, galloped all out for the ranch.

He passed once more through herds of fat cattle with which the Pineapple lands were well stocked but saw no humans at all until he was dismounting in the yard. Then he heard a door bang and saw Sheriff Gus Emmett and his deputy, Branch Argon, leaving Bill Crowe's office. At the same time they saw him. They must have seen the riderless horse too and the limp bundle across Curly's saddle for they came quickly, the fat sheriff waddling, and puffing audibly.

'What's this?' he said.

Dark, lithe Branch Argon did not say anything. He helped Curly lift Klaus from the horse, carry him into the bunkhouse and lay him down.

Then he stood with his thumbs hooked into his belt and said, 'All right, cowboy, talk!'

Gus Emmett, who had followed them, stood there with a very similar pose and Curly thought suddenly that the dark, truculent deputy must look something like Emmett had looked in his younger days.

However, he did not like the man's attitude. He said: 'You don't own this bunkhouse, friend, get out o' my way. I'll go fetch Bill Crowe. Klaus wants seein' to.'

He started forward then paused in his stride as a gun appeared as if by magic in Branch Argon's hand. He could not remember having ever seen such a fast draw before; the man certainly was Emmett all over again.

It was the latter who spoke. 'Better tell us, son,' he said gently. 'Make it quick.'

'He drank from a water-hole which must have been laced with some kind of poison.'

'Where was this?'

'Down at the corner fence – by the hills.'

Footsteps thudded outside. Branch Argon stepped back. His gun dropped into its sheath as quickly as it had been drawn. Both he and the sheriff turned towards the door.

Bill Crowe came in. 'What's going on here?' he said. He saw the still form on the bunk: brushed past the sheriff and his deputy and bent over it.

'He's in a bad way,' he said. He whirled on Curly. 'What happened to him?'

The cowboy told him quickly. Crowe nodded his head. His granite face went even grimmer but no hair of his carefully brushed head, no line of his black broadcloth and snow-white linen seemed to be dishevelled by his haste and his bending.

He wasted no time. 'I'll go get the first-aid chest,' he said. At the door he turned. 'You'd better ride to Ramrod right away, Simpson, and fetch the doc,' he said. 'Just in case—'

'The young man's staying here,' interrupted the sheriff. 'Send someone else.'

Crowe turned on him. His grim face became suddenly contorted: Curly saw the hate in his eyes. Then the expression faded. The boss looked from the sheriff to his deputy and back again.

They returned his look. Branch Argon's hand was in his belt, very near to his gun.

'Don't waste time,' said Gus Emmett.

Without another word Crowe turned. The door banged behind him.

'What do you want with me?' said Curly. 'I've told you what happened.'

'Stay put, sonny-boy,' said Branch Argon and he had his gun out once more.

Curly shrugged and sat down on the edge of his bunk. He looked quizzically up at the deputy.

'You're mighty proud of your draw, ain't you, pard-ner?' he drawled.

Argon flushed until his dark face was almost purple. The barrel of the gun went up and he started forward. Curly got to his feet and balled his fists. He tried to watch the gun and Argon's choleric eyes both at the same time.

He had no wish to be pistol-whipped. Still less did he want to get shot.

'Branch,' said Sheriff Emmett sharply.

The deputy hesitated, the flush subsided. Footsteps thudded outside once more. He did his sleight-of-hand trick and moved away from Curly. His thumbs were hooked into his belt as, with the sheriff, he turned to look at Bill Crowe again.

The boss carried a large black box by a leather strap. His shoulders bulged in his black broadcloth. Although he was no doubt a powerful man he seemed to be having difficulty in carrying his burden. The sheriff gave a jerk of his head, then another, more imperiously. With a sullen look on his face the deputy moved forward to help Bill Crowe.

But the big boss, though not sullen, could be savage. 'Get out of my way,' he snarled. 'I can manage.'

Argon backed away, that dark red flush staining his face once more. With three more long strides Crowe reached his objective and placed the box on the floor beside the bunk where Al Klaus lay. He flung the lid open with a crash and delved inside. Curly moved beside him to give any help which might be needed.

The cowboy looked down at his pardner of the afternoon. During the argument between himself and the law poor Klaus had been forgotten. Now Curly realised with horror that the man's face was beginning to assume a blueish tinge.

Crowe had raked a bottle of brandy from the depth of the black box. He bent over Klaus with this in his hand. He said: 'He certainly looks bad. I've sent Gimpy for the doctor and some more of the boys down to the water-hole. Did you bring the fencing tools back with you?'

The question seemed pointless to Curly. He said: 'No, I left them where they were. I was too worried about gettin' Klaus back to the ranch as quickly as possible to waste time in collectin' 'em.'

'Those tools cost money,' said Crowe harshly. 'They're too expensive to leave lying around where anybody can come along and pick them up..'

'I guess the boys who've gone down there will collect 'em.'

'That's no excuse. You should have brought them back with you.'

Right now Crowe seemed more concerned about his tools than about one of his men who might be dying for all he knew. Curly marvelled at the man.

He tried to make his voice as flat as possible as he said: 'Why not try Klaus with some of that brandy.'

'Are you trying to give me orders?' Crowe almost snarled.

'No, I jest thought—'

'Let me do the thinking. You're paid to work not think.' Crowe pulled the cork from the neck of the bottle. 'See if you can prize his lips open.'

Curly felt a faint repugnance as he inserted his fingers between the tight lips. They met the teeth, which were tightly locked.

'It's like he's got lockjaw,' he said.

Crowe did not answer. He inserted the neck of the bottle between the lips and tilted it slightly. Some of it seemed to run between Klaus's lips but more of it ran down his chin. His face did not change. In sudden alarm Curly dropped his head to the broad chest.

'He's still alive,' he said. 'But only just. What the hell shall we do?'

Both men turned as they heard the door open. Sheriff Emmett had gone outside. He returned quickly.

'Looks like Gimpy an' the doc are coming,' he said.

A few minutes later hooves clattered outside. Then boot-heels scraped. Emmett flung the door open to admit a tall cadaverous man in a broadcloth suit which was almost green with age. He carried the badge of his profession: a little black bag.

He darted little quick glances all around him then without speaking to anybody strode forward to the man on the bunk. Curly and Bill Crowe stood aside out of his way and he bent his long length and peered closely into Klaus's blue face. He lifted his eyelids, tried to prize his teeth apart, even pulled one of his ears.

'He allus pulls their ears,' said Branch Argon. 'That's the only way he can tell whether they're dead or not.'

The doctor did not seem to hear this remark. Curly was still wondering how the hell he could tell by their ears when the tall man said in a neighing voice: 'A stomach-pump is what is wanted here. I'd like a large bowl or a bucket.'

'Get one,' said Bill Crowe over his shoulder.

Curly went through the side door into the lean-to and straight on through the mess-hut to the kitchen.

'What's goin' on back there?' said the cook.

Curly told him briefly that 'Klaus was sick and the doc wanted a bucket or somep'n.' He carried the bucket back into the bunkhouse and the tall doctor got to work gravely with the stomach-pump.

After it was all over Klaus began to stir feebly and moan.

'He's lucky to be able to do that,' said the medico. 'That was a pretty powerful poison he'd got inside of him, whatever it was. Where did he pick it up?'

'From a water-hole,' said Crowe suddenly, savagely. 'Those damn' settlers!'

'What makes you think it was settlers,' said the sheriff.

'Yeh, what makes me think that?' echoed Crowe in a deep thoughtful voice.

He turned abruptly and left the bunkhouse. From outside came the sounds of the men arriving for their early-evening meal.

'Stay here,' said the sheriff to his deputy and he followed in the wake of Bill Crowe.

'Well,' said the tall doctor briskly. 'There isn't much more I can do here. He'll live I guess.' He turned to Curly. 'When your pard finally comes round feed him warm milk and brandy from a spoon. Don't give him any solid food until he's sitting up and taking notice.' He bent like a wooden puppet and delved in his bag and brought forth with a flourish a little black box. He handed this to Curly saying: 'When he begins to eat give him one of these after every meal. If any more complications occur send for me immediately.'

The doctor bobbed suddenly as if one of his strings had snapped. Then he said, 'Good-day, gentlemen,' and swept out of the bunkhouse.

The sound of the other footsteps mingled with that of his. There was a slight scuffle then Bill Crowe burst through the door. He glared at Curly.

'Those tools weren't there when the men got there,' he said. 'Why in hell didn't you bring them?'

'I told you why.'

'If they're not found you'll pay for them out of your wages.' With that parting shot the boss disappeared again.

Curly and the deputy were exchanging their first good-humouredly rueful glances when the door burst open once more and the sheriff came in. 'Where's Crowe?'

'He was here a few minutes ago,' said Branch Argon.

'I must have missed him,' puffed the sheriff. 'I've bin chasing that galoot all over the ranch.'

He turned about again and moved out like a tugboat under a head of steam.

A few minutes later he was back again, more breathless than ever.

'Crowe's took a bunch of boys out huntin' settlers,' he said. 'Ride to town an' get a posse. I'm goin' after them right away.'

CHAPTER TEN

After both lawmen had gone and the frenzied clattering of hooves had faded away in the distance, Curly looked down at Klaus and said: 'You're well out of it this time, pardner.'

The sick man began to babble incoherently in delirium. His voice got stronger all the time.

Finally Curly culled words and phases from his babblings.

'Shoot 'em ... Shoot 'em all ... Only way ...Sweep ... sweep ... burn 'em ....'

None of it made sense. Maybe Klaus too was referring to the settlers. But whether they were malignant or much-maligned Curly could not decide offhand. His father had been a settler; that counted for a lot with him. Should it he wondered; was that fair? Was he turning Bill Crowe and the Pineapple into bogies once more? He looked down at Al Klaus, rolling now with sudden spasms of pain: whoever did that to a man – and to cattle and horses too – ought to be shot.

He decided he ought to get the brandy and milk the doctor had prescribed for the sick man. He turned to make for the kitchen and as he did so the bunkhouse door opened slowly. He turned again, his mouth dropping open slightly as Teresa Crowe came in.

She hesitated on the threshold and said, 'Hallo.'

He said, 'Hallo.'

She came in a little further. 'I heard that a man was sick. I wondered if there was anything I could do.' She wore her white shirtwaist and brown skirt once more. On her feet were small red moccasins. Her movements were light and graceful as she moved nearer to the man on the bunk. She was well-built but right then seemed to Curly to be only a little bit of a thing. He said: 'The doc said to give him brandy an' warm milk when he comes round. I was jest going to get some.'

'I'll watch him,' she said.

'Yeh,' said Curly. 'Yeh.' He turned and went to the mess-hut.

The man in the yellow apron and his pudgy young sidekick were sitting with their feet up smoking. They hit the floor with alacrity as Curly entered.

'Gosh,' said the cook in disgust. 'I thought it was the boss creepin' up on us.'

'I told yuh he'd gone out,' said the boy shrilly. 'Seems like there ain't a soul in the place 'cept us.'

'How's Klaus?' said the cook.

'He's livening up.'

'Anythin' we can do?'

100

'No,' said Curly hastily. 'You have a lounge while you've got the chance. I'll look after him. Right now I want some brandy an' warm milk – doctor's orders.'

'I'll get it,' said the cook.

He opened a cupboard and delved into the bottom of it. He straightened, bringing forth a bottle half full of brandy. He turned swiftly, aiming a swipe at his sidekick's head. The boy dodged it with the ease of practise.

'You've bin at this stuff again,' said the irate cook.

'I ain't.'

'Cut the lip an' put some milk on.'

Curly waited in a fever of impatience. The kitchen staff did not hurry themselves but finally a small saucepan, full of warm milk laced with brandy was ready. Curly took it and retraced his steps to the bunkhouse. He wondered whether the girl, Teresa, would still be there.

She was bending over the bunk with her hand on the sick man's forehead. The pose was a mixture of gentleness and efficiency and it engendered conflicting feelings in the cowboy's mind.

She looked up as he approached. 'He's in a bad way,' she said. 'What happened to him?'

'He drank some poisoned water.'

'Poisoned water?' The girl sounded very puzzled; Curly wished he had not told her.

She went off on a new tack. 'Why have my uncle and all those men ridden out?'

'I don't rightly know, Miss. I'm still kind of a stranger here.'

'Has it something to do with this man?'

'I guess so.'

'Was it a poisoned water-hole he drank from?'

Involuntarily Curly answered, 'Yes.'

'Oh, why won't they let it be—?' The girl broke off suddenly. She leaned nearer to Klaus. The man was mumbling again.

'Stop 'em … drive 'em out … burn 'em.'

'The theme-song of the Pineapple Ranch,' she said bitterly.

Her face was set now in a hard mould. For a moment she looked very much like her uncle – and Curly did not like it.

Klaus stopped mumbling. His mouth was slightly open. The girl said: 'Give me that spoon.'

Her voice was imperious. Mechanically he handed her the spoon. He held the saucepan while she dipped the spoon into it then conveyed the brandy and milk to Klaus's mouth. The man took it down. The girl did the job with a severe efficiency and again Curly was irritatingly reminded of her uncle.

Klaus's colour was coming back. He sucked thirstily at the brandy and milk but did not open his eyes. Finally he was still.

'He's sleeping,' said the girl. 'I think he'll be all right now.'

Curly turned away and put the saucepan on the corner of the table. The girl followed him and placed the spoon beside it. She looked directly at him. She said: 'I never thanked you properly for coming to my rescue this afternoon.'

'It was nothin', I jest happened to be the nearest. Anyway, you certainly gave that hoss a run for his money. He's as docile as a baby now.'

'Yes, but I shan't be allowed to ride him again. Uncle was furious.'

Curly had nothing to say to that. She held out her hand. 'Thank you, Mr—'

She paused. He took her hand. 'Simpson's the name, Miss. Joe Simpson. Most folks call me Curly.'

He held her hand and she was very close to him. He remembered the warmth and softness of her out in the grass, the feel and the scent of her. She was looking up at him and her dark eyes were unfathomable. She tried to draw her hand away and half-unconsciously he held on to the soft warmth of it. In doing so he pulled her closer to him. Next moment his other hand had gone around her shoulders. He drew her gently close to him and kissed her.

For a moment her lips were soft on his. Then they became hard, he felt her teeth: with surprising strength she wrenched herself away from him.

She swung the door open, went out and banged it shut, leaving him gaping.

He felt a fool. Then, on top of that, he felt a cad. Did the fact that he had, maybe, saved the girl's life give him the right to make love to her?

Her reactions he had had no time to define. First they had been good, then they had been bad. They had been mighty quick both ways!

He was piqued – and then he became savage. Maybe she had just been playing with him. If she was anything like her uncle he figured that was just what she would enjoy doing.

He could not make up his mind about anything. This territory and the people in it were rapidly getting him hog-tied. He felt like going out and saddling his horse and riding away from it all.

But he did not. He pulled up a chair to the side of Klaus's bunk and sat down. He made himself a cigarette and sat and smoked while the sick man slept like a baby beneath him.

Long after the light had gone Curly sat smoking in the darkness, the red spot of his cigarette throwing a faint glow around him. He was like that when he heard footsteps and the door opened. He did not move. He did not give a cuss who it was.

But ti was only the cook, come to see how Klaus was getting on. Curly roused himself. 'He's all right,' he said. 'I guess we ought to leave him for a while.'

He followed the cook back into the mess-hut and had his belated early-evening meal. The ranch was as quiet as the grave.

After the meal Curly's inactivity began to irritate him. He lit another cigarette and strolled out into the yard. His footsteps took him over to the corral where the white stallion still browsed. Curly clicked his tongue and the beast came over to him, let him stroke his nose, nuzzled his shoulder.

'You're all tuckered out now, ain't yuh, ol' feller,' said the cowboy.

He left the horse and his steps then led him past Bill Crowe's office, towards the ranch-house. The white verandah was before him when he halted, listening. Faintly on the soft breeze came the sound of galloping hooves.

Curly turned and walked back towards the bunkhouse. The horses came on at a furious rate. There was no shouting, there was a strangeness which communicated itself to Curly so that, on the spur of the moment he darted back into the cover of Bill Crowe's cabin.

The horsemen came on without any slackening of speed, Curly saw them as they passed the corral. About nine of them in all. He knew then that they were not Pineapple men. Were they maybe the posse from town?

Logic told him they were not. They would be out in the badlands after Crowe and his men. Even so, when the shooting started he was taken by surprise. The horses were prancing and the men were shooting at the bunkhouse and the mess-hut. From the latter came the sudden boom of a shotgun. The cook had opened up.

Curly saw a man pitch from his horse. The rest milled a little. It seemed like they were taken by surprise. Some wheeled and rode out of harm's way. Others dismounted and took cover. One ran within a few yards of Curly and squatted down behind a barrel in front of the verandah of the ranch-house. Curly, hidden in the shadows, let him go.

The cowboy watched another man who, squatting behind a wagon with a broken wheel, was lighting a torch. Curly drew his gun.

The man, his torch well alight, rose with it swinging in his hand. Curly fired.

The man gave a yelp of agony. The torch fell from his hand and spluttered on the ground. He grasped his upper arm and crumpled up behind the wagon. In the sudden hush Curly could hear him sobbing with pain.

A man shouted. Another one started to blaze away. The cook's shotgun boomed and, with its echo a man said, 'Let's get going.' Then the whole bunch of them were scrambling for their horses.

For a moment Curly had forgotten the existence of the man by the verandah steps. This lapse almost cost him his life as the man rose suddenly and began firing. A slug plucked at Curly's shoulder, another burned the wind past his cheek. Then he was retaliating and the man had got down once more behind his barrel.

Curly had no cover except the deep shadows. Every time he pressed the trigger his position was given away. He was pinned to the side of the cabin like a moth on a card.

The man began to fire again from cover and Curly was kept busy dodging. The man's pards were becoming aware of the position, too. When Curly tried to dodge to the back of the cabin he was received with a hail of fire from them. Although the cook with his shotgun was preventing the attackers from getting too bold, Curly was in a tight corner. The attackers, aware now that the sudden offensive on their flank was the work of only one man, were beginning to wheel once more.

Help came from an unexpected quarter. Curly's eyes almost started from his head when he saw the white figure on the verandah steps. He opened his mouth to shout but the words died in his throat. The shout came from the girl. The man behind the barrel had half turned. Curly fired and at the same time saw the stabs of flame on the verandah. In the background he could hear the cook's gun booming.

He left cover and ran across to the verandah, past the still figure crumpled behind the barrel.

As he climbed the steps he said, 'You all right, Miss Teresa?'

She stood with the smoking gun n her hand. 'I'm all right,' she said. 'I guess that puts us square, uh?'

She turned swiftly and disappeared into the house.

Curly paused then spun savagely on his heels, his gun ready. The sound of galloping hooves came to him again, fading rapidly, then swelling again. He ran forward; he saw the cook come out of the mess-hut and he realised that the attackers were running and another larger band of horsemen were approaching.

He ran to the man behind the barrel and grabbed his shoulder. The man sagged. Although Curly could not see his face he had no doubt that he was dead.

He ran on to the bunkhouse and as he approached the door the horsemen were reining in and dismounting. Curly recognised the fat sheriff and his deputy and Sam Hobel and Bill Crowe and the surly hatchet-faced Hank. He saw the cook running towards them. Then he opened the bunkhouse door and went inside. He found the lamp and lit it.

The place was a shambles. There was no glass in any of the windows: it was strewn in jagged pieces all over the floor. The wall opposite to the windows was peppered. Curly crossed swiftly to the bunk where Klaus lay and was relieved at what he saw. Klaus was still sleeping gently, like a child.

A few feet above his head, in the wall behind was a line of bullet-holes. If Klaus had been sitting up his head would have been cut to pieces.

'You're well out of it again, pardner,' said Curly softly.

He turned as the door opened. Bill Crowe came in.

'What happened, Simpson?' he barked.

Curly told him. Crowe heard him out with growing rage and when he had concluded said: 'And you don't know who they were?'

'Didn't have the faintest idea. I got one of 'em though.' Curly thought it wisest to keep the girl's name out of it: she'd tell her uncle about the incident if she wanted to.

He went on: 'I got two of 'em really. One of 'em in the arm. He got away. The other one's lying behind a barrel near the ranch-house. The cook put in some good work with his shotgun. I don't know whether he got anybody or not.'

'He ain't sure,' said Crowe brusquely. 'Come on – show me that gink.'

He grabbed a spare lantern from a corner and lit it. Curly led him to the man behind the barrel, crumpled up there with the side of his face pressed to the hard wood and iron hoops as if he had gone to sleep in that uncomfortable position.

His eyes were closed, his face red and bloated. His blue shirt was stained with crimson in three places.

'You certainly riddled him,' said Crowe.

He poked a shoulder and the dead man rolled on to his back. Crowe held the lantern above his face so that the features were fully illuminated. He was tubby, seedy-looking. His bloated face was a muddy colour, it looked familiar to Curly. His mind groped.

Suddenly everything came back to him. His first morning in Ramrod City. His entrance into Tiny's place. The man tumbling backwards down the stairs. Helped to his feet by Curly, scuttling for the door.

Curly had not seen the man since that morning. Until now. It was the same man, all right, he was sure of that.

CHAPTER ELEVEN

Later Sheriff Emmett identified him as a saddle tramp who had blown into town a week before Curly. He just loafed around and did not find any work. Then a few days ago, he disappeared altogether.

'He was the kind of a man who could be hired to do any kind of dirty work I guess,' said the fat man.

'Who hired him this time?' said Bill Crowe harshly.

'We don't know that – yet.'

Gus Emmett, Branch Argon, and the posse from town, despite black looks from the Pineapple staff, continued to hang around.

Curly learned that the two parties had clashed in the badlands and a gun-battle had been narrowly averted. Furthermore no sign had been found of any settlers or the missing tools. The only find was that of two carcasses, steers who had obviously taken a drink at the poisoned water-hole and then crawled away to die.

Klaus awoke, a well man, and told his story, thus exonerating Curly from all blame.

111

No more clues were found towards the identity of the people who attacked the ranch though it was generally assumed that they were the same who had cut the wire, poisoned the water-hole, and stolen the tools.

Bill Crowe had changed his tune. He put no blame now on the hated townsmen. As the law-party, with the body, finally rode off the boss shouted after Gus Emmett.

'Don't come back here till you've done something about this. I'll give you a couple of days then I'll start to move on my own.' The sheriff made no reply. The jeers of the cowhands floated after the townsmen until they disappeared into the night.

The following morning many of the men were kept back from the range to clean up and repair the damage done by the nocturnal raiders. Curly was quite the hero of the hour and was compelled to recite his tale over and over again. He hoped Bill Crowe, who gave no sign, was as proud of him, and the lost tools would be forgotten. But he had to admit that it was probably a forlorn hope.

Dave Grinewold and he were working together in the bunkhouse when Sam Hobel came in and called them over to him.

'I want you boys to hitch up the buckboard an' go into town,' he said. 'Here's a list of the things you've got to bring.'

He handed them a paper. 'There'll be a lot of glass. Take care of it. An' keep outa trouble.'

They reached Ramrod City just before noon to find it sweltering in the sun. Dirty and somnolent; very few people in the street but quite a few lounging in the shadows of the boardwalk on one side where the sun did not strike. Curly could almost feel the eyes watching them as they passed along the main drag.

'Phew,' said Dave. 'That was some drive. I vote we go get a drink before we do anything else.'

'I'm with you,' said Curly, who had the reins.

He halted the horses outside Brodie's and they got down from the box and entered the place. They stopped just over the threshold to get their eyes accustomed to the gloom after the sun-glare outside. They mopped their streaming faces with their bandannas.

The place was pretty full. The buzz of talk died and all heads were turned towards them. Then as they walked to the bar the habitues got on with their drinking – but it seemed to Curly that there was a subtle new quality, almost a menacing one, in the new hum of chatter. Still, maybe that was just his overworked imagination again.

They had a couple of drinks apiece from the sullen-faced bartender then went out once more into the sunshine.

'The store is just down the end of the block,' said Dave. 'We can walk that far.' He called the horses and the patient beasts plodded alongside them as they went along the boardwalk.

As they passed Tiny's boarding house a girl came

out and almost ran into them. Curly had a confused impression of black curls, a bronzed vivacious face, bright dark eyes, a light flowered dress.

Dave doffed his hat and said, 'Good morning, Mary.'

The girl said 'Good morning' frigidly and then passed them.

'That's Mary Brookes, Tiny's niece,' said Dave.

'Oh, Tiny's got a niece, too, has he?'

'Shore has.' Dave grinned. 'Though I guess she don't like Pineapple boys no more'n her uncle does.'

'Why doesn't her uncle like 'em?'

It seemed to Curly that Dave hesitated a mite before he answered. 'I guess it's because the Pineapple owns so much stock around here. Tiny's a big man, maybe he thinks he's bein' crowded.' There was sardonic humour in the dark, dapper man's voice. Curly figured that Dave Grinewold could be a nasty customer if need be. He was probably pretty unscrupulous too: there was the same hardness about him which characterised most of the Pineapple boys.

If there was any 'crowding' to be done, they were the boys to do it. Curly began to understand something of the townsfolks' resentment.

He began to think about this Mary Brookes, Tiny's niece, and found himself contrasting her in his mind with Bill Crowe's niece, Teresa. Then things got jumbled. He figured he'd have to see more of this Mary before he could get things really straightened out. Right now Teresa was in the dog-house: he could not figure *her* at all.

They reached the store, entered, and were greeted with the usual surliness by the bespectacled old goat behind the counter.

Dave gave him the list they had from Sam Hobel. He grunted and peered at it, then turned and disappeared into the gloom behind.

'We oughta get all we want from here,' said Dave. 'Then we'll get goin'. I hate this place – particularly in the day time when the townsfolk are top-dog. These damn' yokels give me the creeps.' After a pause he went on: 'Mind you, there's a bunch of us ridin' in here tonight when there'll be more doin'. *Me*, I've got a date with a woman – but most of the boys'll just be horsing around. Like to come along?'

'Yeh, sure,' said Curly instantly.

The shopkeeper returned staggering under a load of sheet-glass. The two men took it from him, carried it outside and tied it to the buckboard. Then they returned to collect the rest of the stuff. The old man was a bit more affable after they had paid him. He wished them 'Good-day' and they went out and climbed on to the box of the buckboard.

'Good-day, Ramrod City,' said Dave sardonically, and flicked the reins.

The horses started up. He urged them to a faster pace.

They were passing Brodie's place when a trio of youths came out of the alley beside it and began yelling 'Pineapple killers', and other things, and throwing rocks. One struck Dave Grinewold on the

shoulder, others smashed into the glass on the buckboard.

The little dark man's face became suffused with
crimson. He twisted in his seat and drew his gun.
Curly saw his teeth bared, his eyes glaring. Then
before he could prevent it Dave fired. The youths
scattered for cover.

Curly grabbed his pardner's arm and jerked it
upwards. The next shot went into the air.

'Quit it, yuh fool, they're only kids!'

Dave subsided and sheathed his gun. People were
pouring from Brodie's place.

'All right,' he snarled. 'But look at 'em. Just look
at 'em. I oughta blast away into the middle of the
whole damn' bunch.'

He climbed into the back of the buckboard.
'There are a couple o' sheets o' glass ruined. We'll
hafta get some more I guess. Who's gonna pay for
this, that's what I want to know?'

People were shouting threats from the sidewalk.
Curly could see by the look of them that they were
the worst element of Ramrod City. He ignored them
as he guided the buckboard around. He did not
think any of them were capable of starting any actual
trouble. The rock-throwing youths were nowhere to
be seen. They had definitely been scared off.

Sheriff Gus Emmett came waddling down the
street.

'What's all the shooting?'

Dave Grinewold told him and he did not mince his
words. In fact he was downright insulting.

The sheriff said mildly: 'You'd better get what you want an' then hit the trail. I don't want any trouble.'

'Horsefeathers,' said Dave rudely.

Again Curly marvelled at the old gunfighter's tolerance as Emmett shrugged and turned away to shoo the milling bystanders back into their holes. Curly was thankful the whip-like deputy, Branch Argon, was not in the office or they would have probably had a gunfight on their hands.

They returned to the store and picked up some more glass. The main drag was pretty quiet as they left it and hit the trail to home. To Curly it seemed like a pall of brooding disquiet hung over Ramrod City. He said to his companion: 'You still aimin' to come back here tonight?'

'Yeh, why not?' Dave almost snarled. 'Them yokels don't scare me. You can stay away if you want to.'

Curly ignored the half-insult. 'I'll come along,' he said.

They drove on in silence to meet a tirade from Bill Crowe when they reached the ranch.

The Pineapple boys rode into Ramrod City in force that night. Besides Dave and Curly there was Hank, Al Klaus (who had made a marvellous recovery) and four other men labelled Artie, Moe, Lobo and Kim. They were a pretty hard-looking bunch and when they walked into Brodie's a sudden hush fell over the place. Chairs scraped, men straightened up as if they expected trouble.

The eight men found places at the bar with little

difficulty. They ordered drinks in jocular voices, making it plain that they were there for a good time.

After the first couple Dave said, 'Wal, boys, I'll go meet my sweetie.'

This was greeted with ribald laughter, which was redoubled when long-faced Hank said: 'Me too.'

However, he followed Dave out and Curly learned that the hatchet-faced man did indeed have a 'date'. Well – you could never tell with women.

After a time the crowd in Brodie's began to get noticeably less.

'What's up?' said Curly. 'Are we scarin' 'em off?'

'Naw,' said the man called Lobo who had somewhat the long lean hungry appearance of a lobo wolf. 'There's a dance on at the meeting-hall. I guess it's started now. Like to come along?'

'I ain't done no hoofin' in years,' said Curly. 'But I don't mind trying my steps again.'

He felt jolly, willing to be friends with everybody. He felt better now than he had felt since he came to this burg.

Finally the whole bunch decided to try out their steps and they trailed down to the huge, barn-like frame building at the bottom of the main street.

In the lobby there was a slight altercation because Lobo and Al Klaus did not like the idea of checking in their guns. They were smoothed down by Curly and the other three men. Each received a check for their hardware and passed through the swinging doors into the dance-hall.

The place was fairly packed. On chairs at the back

a six-piece band was sweating in the heat while a thin man in shirtsleeves and red suspenders stood on a box and called out the numbers.

The six cowboys stood a little self-consciously on the edge of the dance-floor and tried to ignore the speculative glances which were thrown at them.

Curly looked around him. Then he stopped looking as he found the person he realised he had been, half-unconsciously, seeking. She was dancing with a tall, set-faced man in black broadcloth. Her hair was piled elaborately on top of her head and shone like black oil beneath the light. Her vivacious face was turned up towards her partner's and she was laughing with a flash of white teeth. She wore a long blue gown which showed a lot of her firm golden neck and her plump golden arms. She danced like she loved doing it, her whole body dancing, her face, her eyes.

Curly watched her entranced and did not notice his companions moving away from him one by one until only Klaus was left.

The dark blocky man, who had followed Curly around like an elder brother as if to show his indebtedness to him, said: 'I know some girls here. Want me to introduce you to anybody?'

Curly started. 'No, thanks, Al,' he said. 'You go an' show your paces. I'll jest browse.'

The dance finished and Klaus moved into the crowd in search of an unattached female. In the meantime Curly was watching Mary Brookes. With her hand resting lightly on her companion's arm she

119

was moving from the floor. What was that tall sad-faced gink to her, Curly wondered. He was old enough to be her father.

He saw another man accost the subject of his speculations. The tall man said a few words to the girl, bowed slightly then moved off with the other man. Curly began to worm his way through the crowd.

The girl was still unattached when he reached her and, as he did so, the band began to play another tune, a waltz. Curly thanked his lucky stars it was a waltz. Now there was not so much danger of his making a fool of himself. He blocked the girl's way, bowed, and asked if he might have the honour.

Her black finely-pencilled eyebrows rose a little. Her dark brown eyes were still dancing. She did not hesitate long before she said 'Yes' and moved into his arms.

At first he was a little clumsy. But not for long. It was almost impossible to be clumsy with this girl. She danced like thistledown.

CHAPTER TWELVE

After a moment she said: 'Haven't I seen you before?'
Her voice was musical, a little husky.

'You passed me this morning. I was with Dave
Grinewold.'

'Dave Grinewold?— Oh, I know; the dark young
man from the Pineapple.' Her voice seemed to go
suddenly flat. Curly awaited the inevitable question.

It was forestalled, indirectly, by him, for he
suddenly saw Carrots on the edge of the floor and
raised his hand in a salute, which the little squint-
eyed man returned.

The girl said: 'You know Carrots then?'

'Yeh.'

'But you're a stranger in town, aren't you?'

'Yes.' Curly took the bull by the horns. 'I came in a
few days ago. I met Carrots at your uncle's place—'

'You know who I am then?'

'Yes, Dave Grinewold told me.'

'You know my uncle?'

'Yes, he did me a favour. But afterwards I did something which he didn't like.'

'What was that?'

'I got a job with the Pineapple Ranch.'

The girl stiffened a little. 'I guessed that was what you were going to say.'

Curly bored on. 'I guess your uncle wouldn't like you to be dancing with a Pineapple man. I don't know why. I don't know what's wrong between the townsfolk and the ranch men. I'm just a wandering cowhand. I was after a job. I got one at the only place, I guess, I could in this territory. I'm doing it to the best of my ability. That's all.'

'You can take that chip off your shoulder, cowboy,' said the girl coolly. 'I don't like the Pineapple administration any more than most but I'm not prejudiced against a man just because he works for those people. A cowhand's got to live the same as everybody else.'

'Bless you for that, Miss—'

'You know the name I think.'

'Miss Mary— Let me introduce myself. Joe Simpson. My friends, for obvious reasons, call me Curly.'

'You talk quite smartly – for a cowboy.'

He could see she was bantering him and he grinned.

She went on: 'Funny thing – at college they used to call me "Curly".'

'The only college I ever went to—'

'Yes, I know, the great open spaces, the stars, the crying of little dogies.' Laughter bubbled in her voice.

122

'Don't let it throw you, Curly. They didn't teach me much at college, except maybe how to dance.'

'They certainly did that. I guess that's the college I ought to've attended.'

'You could do with a few lessons,' she said.

'Would you like to step out? Take a walk maybe—'

'Keep right on dancing, cowboy,' she replied firmly. 'I can stand it if you can.'

She stood it so well that when that dance finished he prevailed upon her to let him have the next one, which she did. At the end of this one, however, she looked at the tiny jewelled watch which was pinned to her breast, and said it was time to go.

'Can I escort you?' he said.

'You'd better not,' she told him.

'But – alone – will you be all right?'

'This isn't Tombstone. Anyway, a carriage will be waiting outside for me, driven by one of my uncle's men. Adios, Curly.'

'Can I—?'

She interrupted him. 'Maybe we'll meet again.' Then with another wave of her hand she was gone, leaving him in a daze.

A few minutes later he was joined by Carrots who grinned his snaggle-toothed grin and said: 'Doin' all right for yuhself, ain't yuh?'

'How come?'

'Mary Brookes, Tiny's niece, she's real quality.'

'What do you know about her?'

'Nothin' much 'cept she comes from Austin. Spends a lot o' time every summer with Tiny. She's a nice kid. She's too nice for a Pineapple boy.'

Curly lost his temper. 'What d'you think gives you the right to—'

Carrots interrupted hastily. 'Sorry, pardner. I guess I shouldn't've said that. I didn't mean it personal y'understand?'

'All right.' Curly was mollified. He looked about him, 'Say, cain't a feller get a drink in this place?'

'Nothin' but weak punch. Let's go over to Brodie's.'

'All right.' They went into the lobby and collected their guns and tramped on up the main drag. Curly wondered whether any of his pards had seen him with Carrots and whether there would be any repercussions this time.

They were both thirsty and they both drank fast and had plenty. Curly began to realise he could stand more than the little man; they talked and gradually he led the conversation around to the subject he desired. Finally he asked a direct question.

'What exactly have you – and everybody else here I guess – got against the Pineapple people?'

Carrots' owlish manner dropped from him. Curly expected a rebuff. But the little man was still very drunk – and garrulous. He began to talk and, despite his condition, there was a deep-seated bitterness in his voice.

'The Eastern federation which owns the Pineapple owns most of the town too. They bought the land on which the town stands. People had to either sell or get out. Most o' the storekeepers an' people here ain't owners, they're lessees or managers an' they pay rent, a good cut of their profits, to the federation. The federation's powerful. It hires men like Bill Crowe, who's a dyed-in-the-wool sidewinder and he in his turn can hire the toughest cowhands. They do everythin' he tells them because he pays them well – if they kick nasty things happen to 'em. If they leave they can't get a ranny's job any place else in the territory.

'The townsmen kick, yeh, but they ain't powerful enough and they ain't got any real leader. Crowe's got power over his men – him an' that vicious buzzard, Sam Hobel – an' he can allus get reinforcements if he wants 'em: men who are allus willing to sell their gun to the highest bidder. Mind you, there's some ordinary decent cowhands at the Pineapple – but not many. An' they don't stay that way for long. Just like somep'n unpleasant happens to them. They become Crowe men eventually, or they hightail. Strange accidents, maybe, happened to folks in town who held out too long. That was 'fore your time, Curly ... 'fore your time ...' Carrots' voice died off into a mumble.

He turned away from Curly and grabbed the bottle of rye in two shaky hands. He slopped some into his glass.

'You're tippin' too much of that stuff into yuh, pardner,' said Curly.

'Think nothing' of it, pardner,' burbled Carrots.

However, he turned away from the brimming glass and leaned nearer to Curly. He said thickly:

'They're burying Kruger tomorrow. The townsfolk are burin' him – imagine that: townsfolk burying a Pineapple man. You comin' to the funeral, Curly?'

'I might.'

Carrots seemed to forget his question. He went on: 'Kruger wasn't a bad feller. But he was finished: he was finished months ago. He'd bin with the Pineapple longer than Hobel. Hobel hated him for it. He'd bin there too long – he knew too much – an' he was no good to them any more ... Yeh, yeh, they're burying Kruger tomorrow. Everythin' cut an' dried. I guess Gus Emmett knows what he's doing—' After that last cryptic sentence Carrots lapsed into silence once more. He turned and lifted his drink. More of it ran down his chin, his shirt-front, and slopped on to the floor than he managed to get into his mouth.

Curly let him be. The little man turned again, leaning on the bar, his head on one side, his squint eyes as owlish as it was possible for them to be.

'Any questions?' he said like a speaker at a public meeting.

Curly asked the question he'd been wanting to ask.

'Tiny? Does Tiny's place belong to these federation people?'

Carrots shook his head vigorously. 'No, sir! Tiny's the fly in the ointment. He's pretty powerful too – in his own tinpot way. An' the Pineapple boys can't boycott his place like they boycotted lots of others – until the folks saw the light. It's the only eating-place in town, everybody uses it. He's got plenty folks lodging with him too. He can afford to boycott Pineapple men – which is a smack in the eye for Crowe. I'm afraid Tiny ain't gonna get away with it for long—' Carrots stopped talking.

Curly said: 'You're a townsman ain't yuh? How did you come to get mixed up with the Pineapple?'

Carrots startled him by giving out with a sudden harsh neighing laugh. His face was working as he turned it towards the cowboy once more.

'I wanted a job badly. So badly that I sold myself for thirty pieces of silver—' Carrots voice became shrill. 'Then I saw the light – that's what the sky-pilots say ain't it?' He gave that neighing laugh once more. 'I quit. I quit—'

Curly stood aghast as Carrots began to tear at his clothes. But the little man was only feverishly undoing the buttons on his shirt-front. Finally he bared his chest.

'I quit. An' look what happened to me. I'm a Pineapple man no more but I'm still wearing their brand!'

A feeling of pity, mixed with a faint repugnance, came over Curly as he looked at the little man's bony chest. It was sprinkled finely with ginger hairs, except for a patch in the centre where the Pineapple brand gleamed sorely.

'I didn't know, Carrots,' he said. 'I guess—'

The words died in his throat as the little man covered himself up again, turned blindly and made for the door.

For some moments after Carrots had disappeared Curly stood looking at the door. Men looked at him strangely. Most of the looks were not pleasant, though it was doubtful whether anybody had clearly seen the incident which took place between the two men.

Curly turned back to the bar, his head bent. He tossed off a drink savagely and poured himself another. Dave Grinewold came up to him. Curly wondered whether he had seen Carrots.

They were still there when the rest of the boys, with the exception of Hank, joined them. There were more drinks and Dave recounted gleefully his adventures with the girl. It seemed to Curly suddenly that there was something jeering and spiteful about the dapper young man. He felt like pushing his face in. Maybe he had been too easygoing. Maybe it was time he went on the prod!

He was, however, still a little muddled when he saddled up with the rest of them and rode out of town. They had decided not to wait for Hank. Maybe the hatchet-faced man had decided to spend the night there.

Curly slept fitfully that night. Before his eyes all the while he could see reddish flesh with the cruel brand of the Pineapple burnt deeply into it.

When he awoke he felt unusually savage and morose. The loud grating voice of Sam Hobel telling everybody to 'look alive' did not help matters.

He dressed himself, stood in a queue to wash at one of the pumps then joined the stream to the mess-hut. He learnt then that Hank had not yet returned from town.

When chow was over the hatchet-faced ranny had still not put in an appearance and Sam Hobel was hopping mad.

As they were moving off most of the boys were surprised to see Sheriff Emmett ride into the yard. So soon – and alone too. He went over to Bill Crowe's office, rapped on the door and entered.

Almost immediately the boss came out and yelled for Sam Hobel, who came a-running.

Curly's job that morning was on the look-out at the 'pineapple' rocks with Dave Grinewold. The latter, as jocular as he was the night before, said that Hobel was just breaking him in – but that Hank would be furious when he got back and discovered that somebody else had his job.

Curly said he didn't give a damn, and why a place like the Pineapple should need look-outs he could not figure.

Dave was noncommittal. He said a powerful spread always had sneaking enemies – why, look at the raid the other night. Curly should be the first to admit the Pineapple needed look-outs.

'Maybe I ain't used to the habits o' this territory,' grunted Curly surlily.

Dave lit a cigarette and became silent. Curly was glad of that. He wanted time to think. His head was spinning from last night's booze: he could hardly get the events of the evening into their proper order. Carrots' tale and the incident which followed it had made an impact on him but now the shock was dying he could remember other things and, in particular, the dance and Mary Brookes.

He remembered what Carrots had said about her and wondered why she had bothered to be friendly with a cowhand like him – and a Pineapple man to boot. Then he got savage again and told himself he was too damn modest and that folks took advantage of his modesty and good nature.

Maybe the girl had only been playing with him. What did he expect her to do: it had been a dance, hadn't it? Anyway, she played in a mighty nice way. And that's all there was to it.

He thought about her all morning and his temper became more mellow. He saw Teresa Crowe riding in the distance.

It seemed like his ponderings had made him hungry for when a couple of men came to relieve them for the midday break he was ready for chow.

But the news the two men brought them knocked the bottom out of his stomach.

Hank had been found in an alley in Ramrod City stabbed to death, the weapon beside him. It was the pair of wire-cutters which had been stolen from by the poisoned water-hole.

CHAPTER THIRTEEN

In the mess-hut Curly and Dave learnt more. The sheriff and Bill Crowe had had high words and the boss had ordered the lawman off the place. He had also threatened that if something was not done soon about the outrages, of which the murder of Hank was the culmination, he would take the law into his own hands.

'You'd like to do that wouldn't you, Bill?' Gus Emmett had said before he rode away.

'Gosh, I thought the boss was gonna draw on him,' said one cowhand over a dish of stew.

Rumours were tossed back and forth. It was said that the sheriff was holding the town-girl who had been with Hank that night.

'No woman did that job,' said a man scornfully.

A belated diner came into the mess-hut. 'I've heard somep'n new,' he said. 'It seems the sheriff's got a line on the man Curly winged in the arm the other night. I heard the boss telling Sam Hobel outside the barn just now. They didn't know I was listening.'

'Better hide yourself, Punchy,' said another man who sat by the window.' Here they are an' they're comin' this way.'

'Bill Crowe never comes in here among all us common cow-herders,' said somebody.

Laughter followed this sally. Nevertheless the man who brought the news hunched himself into a furthermost corner and tried to look like he wasn't their any more.

The mess-hut door was flung open and Sam Hobel strode in. Behind him stalked broad, stooping, fault-lessly-dressed Bill Crowe.

'Quiet,' yelled the foreman, then, as the babble died: 'The boss wants to say a few words to yuh.'

Crowe strode forward then and Hobel effaced himself against the closed door.

'I've only a few words to say,' said Crowe. 'But I want you to listen to them carefully an' abide by them. You know what'll happen if you don't.' He paused. Nobody said anything. He went on: 'I want every man to keep away from Ramrod City tonight. Or any other night .... I'll tell you when you can go. Is that understood?'

Nobody answered him. Evidently it was under-stood. He turned his back on them. Hobel opened the door for him and he stalked out. The foreman cast a last pregnant look into the bunkhouse then closed the door behind them.

The man in the window watched. Finally he said 'They've gone in the office.'

Immediately the buzz of talk became a deafening chatter. The general opinion was that the boss had 'something up his sleeve' – but what that something was made speculation rife and almost violent.

Curly Simpson had a bellyful of these braying jack-asses and went outside for a quiet smoke. A few moments later Dave Grinewold joined him.

'Looks like we'll be seein' some action soon, Curly, me boy,' he said, 'if that fat slob of a sheriff don't liven up his ideas.'

'I guess a man like Gus Emmett knows what he's doin'.'

'Don't you bank so much on that. Gus Emmett ain't Gus Emmett any more. He wouldn't get by as much as he does I guess if it wasn't for that fast-shootin' deputy of his. He's just plumb lazy – the line o' least resistance is his motto. The boss oughta take over the town an' put in his own law-officer.'

Dave shut up then and looked around him as if he thought somebody had been eavesdropping. He assumed the clam-trap which was a characteristic of the Pineapple boys.

They were joined by more of the bunch and were still smoking when Sam Hobel came out of the office and began to shout at them to 'quit lounging about an' get back to their jobs'.

'He shore is a slave-driver,' grumbled one man. 'I figure we got another ten minutes to go yet.'

However, he did not argue the point with the foreman. Curly smiled sardonically. He was beginning to have a healthy hate for most of these men. But this did not override his feelings for the vicious beanpole of a foreman. Hobel was a freak. He knew it and he gloried in the fact, just as he gloried in the power he had over these cowboys.

Dave and Curly got their horses and adjourned one more to their look-out post on the 'pineapple' rocks.

The days passed and things were pretty quiet. If the law visited the ranch again the boys did not learn of it. From their post Dave and Curly saw very little traffic except that of browsing steers and their own men passing to and fro. They saw Teresa Crowe from time to time. The white stallion still browsed in the corral and she rode a little brown cow-pony. Once she got near enough to see the two men. They doffed their hats and she waved to them.

Curly thought about her, and about Mary Brookes too, until his mind was quite muddled between them. A man had little else to do on these rocks but talk and smoke and think about women and the promise of action. It was a waiting, brooding time, a sultry time before a storm which seemed that it would never come – a prelude to action which degenerated into a mere lying in wait.

At night they sat in the bunkhouse or out by the corral and yarned and gambled or took short walks and smoked. Curly Simpson, who felt like he wanted to get away and be alone, got into the habit of doing the latter. Walking and smoking.

It was the third night after Bill Crowe's pronouncement that Curly's perambulations led him around the back of the bunkhouse. His cigarette made a glow in the darkness and eventually it attracted a white moth which flitted from out of the gloom.

The moth spoke, and Curly almost jumped out of his skin.

'I saw you from my bedroom window. I thought it was you.'

'What made you think it was me?'

'Oh, I dunno. I suppose it's because you're the sort of man I'd expect to walk out in the night alone.'

'Is that a compliment or an insult?'

'Take it as you please.' There was a mocking note in the girl's voice. Then it became serious again. 'I can't think of any other man who'd browse out here like that – except maybe Dave Grinewold.'

'You like Grinewold?'

'He's more gentlemanly than the rest of them – but I don't know him very well. I'm not allowed to know any of the men.'

'I don't profess to be gentlemanly. I'm just a common cowhand like the rest of them.'

'You're not.'

'In what way?'

'Oh, I dunno, you're just different.'

'You flatter me, Miss Teresa. You don't usually talk to me that way.'

'I haven't had much chance.' She came suddenly

closer. 'Don't be mad with me, Curly. I didn't mean to be ornery the other day. It was just that I was scared. I owe you a lot—'

'You don't owe me anythin'. You squared that when you shot that man. Where did you learn to shoot?'

'My uncle taught me.'

'Yeh, they tell me he's quite good at it himself. You're scared of him—?'

'Yes, I am, in a way.'

'He never uses violence to you, does he?'

'He could do I guess. He always has to have his own way.' She looked up at Curly. He could see the faint outlines of her face, her eyes shining in the dark.

She wore her white shirtwaist and skirt. Her neck was arched a little, her breasts high and full.

'Put that cigarette out,' she said. 'He might see us.'

'That really would gum things up wouldn't it?' said Curly sardonically.

The presence of the girl, the scent of her was making his head reel. He was holding himself in. God, she was sweet.

He dropped his cigarette and ground it savagely beneath his heel. Then he caught her around her shoulders and drew her close until her body was pressed hard against his.

'Curly,' she said breathlessly.

He kissed her. He could feel her heart pounding and his own felt like it had come up into his throat and was half-choking him. He slackened his hold and she leaned against him, her head on his shoulder. After a moment she lifted up her head to be kissed once more.

After that she turned, leaned back in the crook of his arm and looked towards the house. It was as if her fear had suddenly returned to her.

This fear was realised when a light flashed on in a back window of the dark bulk. She said: 'I must go' and tore herself away from him.

As she sped away she called over her shoulder, 'The same time tomorrow night.'

A rather dazed Curly, trying hard to be thoughtful, returned to the bunkhouse. He had some decisions to make, some mighty big ones, and fooling around with Teresa Crowe wasn't going to help them none.

The following evening he was forced to make his decisions, as he had known he would have to do sooner or later. The person who brought things to a head was none other than Bill Crowe who, with the foreman in tow, paid another visit to the bunkhouse.

The men had just finished chow and were lounging around chatting and smoking. They sat up when the boss entered. There was an air of expectancy. Crowe did not mince words.

'It seems like nothin's bin done about the murder of Hank, and the other things that have happened to this ranch of late. These things we know have their root in Ramrod City. I propose tonight to ride on Ramrod City. The main objective will be the sheriff's office, Brodie's place, and Tiny Waters' place. That's all I have to say now. You will receive further instructions before you start. Any man who doesn't want to come along can speak his piece right now.'

Nobody spoke for a moment. Then a man shouted, 'We're with you, boss' and others took up the cry.

Something like a smile creased Crowe's granite features.

'You're to be ready in an hour,' he said. 'I don't want anybody to leave the place before then.'

After he had left an excited buzz of conversation arose. Men began to check and re-oil their guns and root out their rifles and shotguns.

Curly pretended to be doing the same but his mind was racing all the time. He knew now what he had to do.

He owed no allegiance to this bunch of cut-throats. But how to get away from them without being spotted, that was the problem.

It was Dave Grinewold who gave him his chance.

The dapper young man came up to him and said, 'Our rifles are in our saddle-boots, ain't they, Curly? What say we go get 'em an' check 'em over?' He added jocularly: 'They might have gone rusty while we've bin sittin' nursing' them up on them rocks.'

'Yeh, they might at that,' said Curly loudly. 'Come on.'

As he followed Dave to the door he wondered why the hell he had not thought of that himself.

One or two of the men asked them where they were going. They were told and made no further comment. Dave Grinewold was a trusted member of the organisation.

The two men made their way to the stables. The yard was silent. a light glowed in the window of Bill Crowe's office, another, very dimly, in the ranch-house up ahead. Curly thought of the girl who would be waiting for him behind that ranch-house. It was almost time now. He felt regret that he would not be able to meet her.

He followed Dave into the stables. From Gimpy's cubby at the back came a faint light. It brightened as the old man opened his door and came out.

'Who's that?' he called. 'It ain't time yet.'

'So he's in the know,' muttered Dave. Then he raised his voice. 'It's jest me an' Curly. We've come for our rifles out of our saddle-boots. Let's have some light will yuh?'

Grumbling to himself Gimpy withdrew but returned almost immediately with a lantern.

Curly was behind Dave. Over the dapper man's shoulder he watched Gimpy. When the limping old man was near enough Curly drew his gun and backed away a little.

'Freeze, both of yuh,' he said. 'I've got you covered.'

Dave stiffened. His hands became claws.

'Don't try anything, pardner,' Curly told him.

Slowly Dave raised his hands above his head. Old Gimpy stood as if petrified.

'Put the lantern down gently on the floor, old-timer,' Curly told him. 'Then straighten up right off an' elevate your paws.'

The old man said, 'What's the idea?' huskily, but he did as he was told.

'A damn' spy,' said Dave Grinewold from between clenched teeth.

'Shut up,' said Curly. He moved forward and reached out for the man's gun.

Dave ducked suddenly and threw himself backwards. Curly had expected something like that. He felt savage satisfaction as he brought the barrel of his gun down on the black bare head. Without a sound Grinewold crumpled up and slumped to the floor.

The old man twitched. 'Stay where you are,' snarled Curly.

He was really on the prod now. He looked around him quickly and pretty soon spotted what he needed: a lariat. He unhooked it from the saddle-pommel. He kept his gun levelled at Gimpy all the time. Finally he said: 'Walk slowly over here and turn around.'

The old man complied. He said: 'You won't get away with this.'

'Shut up. Put your hands behind you.'

He lashed the gnarled wrists with the rope then he jerked. Cursing vilely, the old man rolled on his back. Curly cut the rope and with another length lashed his feet together. Then he gagged him with his own sweat-cloth.

He repeated the process with Dave Grinewold then dragged both of them into Gimpy's cubby. He doused the light in there. He worked fast but found time to stop and think a little. He debated what to do. He could let all the horses free and set the stables on fire. It would have given him the greatest satisfaction to do that. But he realised that inevitably the wrath of the Pineapple would fall on the town.

No, he must let them go through with what they planned, for it would have to come sooner or later. He must ensure that he gave the alarm so that they received a warm reception when they got there.

He unhitched his horse and mounted him. Before he left the place he blew out the lantern. The yard was silent and empty. Nobody challenged him. He walked the paint until he figured they were out of earshot of the ranch then he set him at a gallop.

He was approaching the trail to town when he heard hoofbeats. The sound was in front coming towards him, not behind him as he had expected. He veered his horse, slowed him down a little.

He heard the rider pass at full speed. The hoofbeats died rapidly into the distance as Curly forged onwards.

CHAPTER FOURTEEN

The main street of Ramrod City was pretty empty as he galloped down it. Light streamed from the dives and the honky-tonks. A few people passing along the boardwalk stared after the horseman. He drew to a halt outside the sheriff's office, ground-hitched the paint, took three strides across the sidewalk and rapped on the door.

A shadow passed across the lighted window. A voice said, 'Open it.'

He opened the door. Light hit him in the face. He halted, blinking, his hands dropping to his belt.

'All right, come on in an' don't look so tough,' said the voice.

He saw the sheriff sitting at the desk right opposite him. It was he who had spoken.,

But there were others besides him, besides Branch Argon who stood scowling at his side. The little office seemed to be full of people.

'Come right in, son,' said Gus Emmett. 'Close the door.'

Curly stepped inside, closing the door mechanically behind him. He looked around him at the hard-faced middle-aged men. They were strangers to him but he knew by the look of them that they were gunfighters, that they had something to do with Ramrod City and the Pineapple. He was aware suddenly that, without his help, things were moving to a climax.

A narrow-eyed raw-boned man to the right of him said, 'Who's this fish?'

'He's a Pineapple fish,' said Branch Argon.

'He is, is he?'

'What do you want, son?' said the sheriff and the room was very quiet.

Curly found his voice. 'Bill Crowe's leading his bunch on the town tonight.'

There were startled exclamations from some of the others but Emmett showed no surprise. 'I was expectin' that sooner or later. That's why I invited my friends to come along.' He looked around him then back at Curly. 'Some of them are still lawmen – others have come out of retirement to help an old friend.'

Curly understood and looked around him. He found himself staring once more into the narrow eyes of the big raw-boned middle-aged man.

'That's Marshal Short from Abilene,' said Emmett. 'You may have heard of him.'

'I have,' said Curly. 'Howdy, suh.'

Short grunted. Then, as if he thought it was expected of him, but for no other reason, he said; 'Howdy, son.'

He paused. Then his next question was shot out suddenly. 'Why ain't you ridin' with that bunch?'

'I'm new here. I didn't know what I was getting into when I joined 'em. I've got friends in town.'

Short looked at the sheriff. Both of them seemed satisfied. Yet there was still a chill atmosphere.

Curly said: 'I've got to go an' warn Tiny. His place is their main objective.'

'All right, son. We'll be ready for them when they come.'

As the sheriff spoke, Curly was going through the door. He closed it behind him. He breathed a sigh of relief as he forked his horse once more.

A few seconds later he dismounted outside Tiny's place and ran up the steps into the lobby. Then he stopped dead, looking upwards

Mary Brookes was coming down the stairs. She was clad all in white, a striking contrast to her dark colouring and jet black hair. She stopped when she saw him and she was like a beautiful picture of surprise.

'Where's your uncle?' he said.

'He's in the kitchen, Curly.'

He passed through the lobby. As he did so he said, 'Wait for me, Mary.'

It was a remark, unthinking, thrown over his shoulder. He hardly realised it; it was just the way he felt.

He passed through the lunch-room and people stared at him. Carrots got up at the back and called his name. As he reached the kitchen doorway Tiny Waters' huge frame blocked it. 'I thought I told you—'

Curly interrupted him. 'I quit the Pineapple.'

Tiny's little black eyes sparkled. He hesitated another moment then said, 'C'mon in, pardner.'

He closed the kitchen door behind them, shutting out the babble of talk.

'Somethin's eatin' yuh, ain't it?' he said. 'Spill it.'

A little breathlessly Curly told him. When he had finished Tiny did not waste much time. He clapped the cowboy on the shoulder.

'Stay here, pardner.' He opened the kitchen door and called for Carrots.

The little man came a-running and was quickly told about what was afoot. He then set out for Brodie's bar to give the alarm.

'Everythin's taken care of now,' said Tiny genially 'An' the sheriff's got the toughest bunch of lead-slingin' hellions in the West down there in his office.'

'I know: I've seen 'em.'

'You stay put awhile an' drink that coffee. You're all tuckered out. I'll go into the lunch-room an' give the boys a spiel. I'm thinking Mr Bill Crowe has bitten off a bit more than he can chew this time.'

After the big man had gone Curly remembered Mary. He slipped out. Tiny was still haranguing the customers, with admirable results, when he passed through the lunch-room.

He found Mary sitting on a chair in the lobby.

'I waited,' she said a little sharply. 'What's going on?'

He felt suddenly overwhelmingly grateful that she had chosen to wait. He told her what was happening, and concluded by saying, 'You'd better go to your room an' stay there.'

'I'm staying here,' she said firmly. 'I may be able to help.'

He saw the set of her lips, the tilt of her chin and remembered they had looked the same for a moment when he danced with her. That seemed a hell of a long time ago. It was like they were very old friends. She was the kind of level-headed comrade he would have chosen for such a time.

There was a tramp of bootheels outside as men took up positions. Some came into the lobby and posted themselves at the window. Others went upstairs. Nobody seemed surprised to see the girl: they evidently knew her qualities better than Curly did. Sheriff Emmett could be heard giving orders outside. Marshal Short poked his head into the boarding-house then out again.

Ramrod City became like an armed camp and people waited all night for the alarm and the attack. Nothing happened. Nothing at all.

The following morning Curly Simpson was questioned in the lobby of the boarding house by the sheriff and his pardners, many of whom suspected he had tricked them for some purpose which would perhaps be divulged later.

'I'll go bail for the younker,' said Tiny Waters roughly. 'He's genuine.'

'That's enough for me,' said the sheriff.

But Marshal Short was not so easily appeased.

'Mebbe the young man's got an explanation,' he said. 'I'd like to hear it.'

Curly said: 'I told you how I got away. Mebbe they found Grinewold and Gimpy and, knowing I'd high-tailed, probably to give the alarm, decided to call it off.'

'D'you really think that 'ud stop them? They'd be right behind you.'

'Yeh. Unless they knew the sheriff had a specially-picked bunch of fighting men here waiting f'r them.'

'How could they know that?'

'Crowe had spies in town. I know that although I don't know who they are—' Curly paused.

'Go on.'

'A rider passed me on the trail as I was comin' in. He was ridin' mighty hard.'

'You think he was goin' to warn Bill Crowe?'

'Could be.'

'Yes, could be,' said Short. 'Mebbe that would stop Bill Crowe, mebbe he's learnin' discretion in his old age.' He spoke of the Pineapple boss as if he knew him well.

His narrow eyes quizzed Curly a second longer. Then he turned on his heels.

'Don't leave town, Curly,' said the sheriff, 'or one o' the boys is liable to shoot at you.'

'Gosh, I ain't aimin' to.'

Time passed uneventfully, at least where action was concerned. The rest of that day Curly stayed in or around the boarding house with Carrots and Tiny and, when he could dodge them, with Mary in the lobby.

She seemed to trust him implicitly. He learnt a lot about her and more than once during the day wished there were not so many people about.

After the evening meal when darkness had fallen and things were beginning to hum down at the honky-tonks, Carrots asked Curly to go and have a drink with him. Their steps led them inevitably to Brodie's place.

Word had got around and Curly received a mixed reception. He kidded himself that it was warmer than of yore. As the night grew older he said to Carrots 'Let's find fresh lodgings. I'm sick o' bein' stared at by the same bunch.'

Carrots grinned, said 'all right' and led the way.

They passed into the street, crossed it to the opposite boardwalk. The street was quiet this side until men moved suddenly from the shadows in front of them.

Curly saw the glint of steel and, shouting a warning to Carrots, threw himself sideways. As he hit a log wall with his shoulder the guns were speaking. He heard Carrots cry out, saw him clutch his side. The blatter of gunfire was deafening, the night was lit by lurid flashes. He was dragging at his own gun but his awkward position hampered his movements.

He got his gun out; Carrots was crawling towards him, he leaned and held out a hand and the little man grasped it desperately. More gunfire came and Curly fired back at the flashes in the shadows, the dim figures crouching there. He heard Carrots gasp and the hand that grasped him went limp and fell away.

Curly felt cold fury and began to move along the wall. A slug plucked his shoulder, another brought searing pain to his leg so that it gave way beneath him. He limped and thought 'this is it' and cared nothing but that he should take as many of the attackers with him as possible. He triggered methodically and saw men tumbling and then he knew his gun was empty.

The night was full of gunfire and the street seemed full of men and behind them a voice shouted his name. A high warning cry. He turned swiftly, saw the big man and ducked. He flung his empty gun viciously and saw the man go down. He fell to his knees, pain beating at him, gunfire rising to a devilish crescendo which seemed to beat in his ears, in his head, driving him down – down …

Then suddenly there was no more and men were grouping around him and hands were lifting him to his feet.

'I'm all right,' he said. 'It's just a crease to my leg. Let's get after them.'

'In time, Curly,' said the cool, high voice of Gus Emmett.

They carried him into the lodging house and Mary

came to fuss over him. His leg, as he said, was only creased and the cadaverous doctor put in an appearance and soon fixed that.

'Where's Carrots?' said Curly. 'How is he?'

The doc had just returned from the little man who was in bed upstairs. He had lost a lot of blood and was unconscious. In answer to Curly's next question the doctor merely shook his head gravely.

Curly rose to his feet and tested his weight on his wounded leg. He looked about him. At Tiny, at Gus Emmett, at Branch Argon, Marshal Short and the rest of the lawmen. His head was buzzing with questions and he began to ask them.

From the answers he pieced together what had happened.

Lawmen had been keeping watch on him unobtrusively all night. They had not been far behind when the Pineapple men had attacked and had arrived in the nick of time. Among the dead were Dave Grinewold, 'Lobo', Al Klaus ....

At the mention of his old pard's name, Curly remembered the voice which had warned him. It had sounded familiar: now he knew its origin.

'Klaus was shot in the back,' said the sheriff. 'By one of his own men.'

'He warned me. He figured he owed me a debt I guess.'

The sadness passed, there was work to be done. Curly followed the sheriff and Branch Argon up the stairs.

Emmett said: 'We've got the rest in jail. There was

quite a bunch of 'em – but no Bill Crowe or Sam Hobel. They're waiting for the boys to return I guess. I'm takin' some boys there instead. They're getting ready now. Comin' along?'

'Am I coming along?' Further words failed Curly. His eyes blazed.

The sheriff grinned. Then his face became grave again as they entered Carrots' room. Mary was sitting beside the bed. She looked past the lawman, looked at Curly. There was something in her eyes which made the cowboy's heart bound.

'You all right?'

'Sure, honey.'

She flushed a little. A strangled sound came from the man in the bed. She looked at the sheriff.

'He's trying to talk. He wants pencil and paper.'

The sheriff produced a large notebook from his pants pocket. The deputy handed him a pencil. Neither of them said anything. It was as if it had all been prearranged. Curly was a little puzzled.

The sheriff crossed to the bed. Two thin hands came out and took the notebook and pencil from his fingers. The girl put her hands behind the wounded man's head and gently eased it up. Carrots saw Curly and managed a travesty of a smile. Then he began to scribble laboriously with the pencil.

The girl and the two lawmen moved a little way from the bed. Curly watched the bent head, the trembling scrawling hand, as if fascinated by them. He started forward when the hand fell limp, the head fell back. Carrots was hardly breathing at all, the pad beneath was full of scrawled writing.

'I'll get the doctor,' said Mary and ran from the room.

'There ain't much more to be done,' said the sheriff.

He picked up the pad and the pencil. He looked at the pad and handed it to Curly. The latter, still very puzzled, started to read.

I poisoned the water-hole and stole the tools and killed Hank. I led the raid on the ranch with a bunch of no-goods from town. I hated the Pineapple people for what they done to me. They killed my half-brother, Cyril, he was not their kind. Bugs – they called him....

Here the writing petered out into indecipherable scrawl, but right at the end of it all, as if Carrots knew he had written all that mattered, he had made an effort and scrawled his signature.

'Bugs,' said Curly half to himself. The name echoed in his mind and suddenly he remembered what Al Klaus had told him about Bugs, whom Bill Crowe had made dance with bullets. Klaus had not said what happened to Bugs.

As if answering the unspoken question the sheriff said: 'The Pineapple drove him out. A coupla days later he was found in a gully with his neck broken.'

The doctor came into the room with a rush. He bent over the man in the bed and was suddenly a grotesque figure of suspended animation. Then slowly he drew the sheet up over Carrots' face.

*

The horses moved slowly on sacking-padded hooves. The men leaned forward in the saddles and gentled the beasts with their hands as they moved nearer to the ranch buildings. They approached from the back and then split up into two parties – a large one and a small one.

The large party moved towards the bunkhouse and the rest, three men only, dismounted from their horses and walked to the back of the ranch-house.

The elderly housekeeper was surprised by them in her kitchen but, reassured by the genial visage of Sheriff Emmett led him and his deputy and Curly Simpson to where Bill Crowe and his foreman sat and waited.

'Get back, ma, an' keep quiet,' said Branch Argon, and he kicked the door open.

The two men rose swiftly, transfixed by the light for a moment. They found themselves covered by drawn guns as the three men filed into the room.

Sam Hobel's little wizened face, atop his beanpole body, was suddenly pale and aghast. But his boss's granite-features showed no surprise.

Crowe said: 'What do you want?'

'What do we want he says,' sneered Branch Argon. 'Ain't he the cool one?'

Gus Emmett flicked a paper from his vest-pocket.

'This is a warrant for your arrest, Bill,' he said. 'For, among other things, the murder of Lon Boyles in Abilene five years ago.'

154

A flicker of emotion contorted Crowe's face for a moment.

The sheriff went on: 'You didn't think that rap 'ud catch up with you, Bill. The man who brought the warrant is outside. He and his men are surrounding the bunkhouse, rounding up all the men you have left. You remember Marshal Short, don't yuh, Bill?'

Crowe's face sagged, became suddenly very old. Then it underwent another transformation, working, the eyes blazing; and Curly Simpson turned swiftly as the door behind him opened.

Teresa had a gun in her hand; her red lips were drawn back from white teeth. Curly remembered how she could shoot and he acted. She turned the gun on him as he sprang.

It went off almost in his face. He felt the hot breath of the slug. Then he had hold of her arm, twisting, and the gun fell at his feet. She clawed at him and he spun her around, flinging her away from him.

The room exploded into violent action.

Bill Crowe's hand snaked across his belly. His draw was very fast, but it was a hopeless chance. Branch Argon shot him clean between the eyes and smiled as he did it.

Sam Hobel went for his gun and the sheriff drew. For a moment Curly was bewildered by the speed of it all. With a cry the girl flung herself across the room to her uncle's body. She was in the way of the sheriff and his deputy.

Sam Hobel raised his gun, swerved, grinning

wolfishly. Then his eyes met Curly's, surprise flashed into them, the gun was raised. Curly triggered twice, coolly, and watched him crumple and die.

He sheathed his gun and looked around him and at the sobbing girl. He felt suddenly beaten and flat and he wanted peace. He went slowly out into the hall, passing men without a word as they came in, not answering them as they told him the Pineapple men were rounded up.

It all passed and as they left the ranch he asked the sheriff a question.

The old gunfighter replied, 'There were faults on both sides, son. There usually is. Experience has taught me tolerance. But this time I almost had too much.'

The sheriff turned as Marshal Short hailed him.

Curly Simpson rode on alone, just an ordinary cowboy, moving forward to the girl who awaited him.